DRIVEN TO KILL SERIES **BOOK 2**

ROAD TO NOWHERE

KATHY SIMON

LARGE PRINT EDITION

Publishing Services provided by Paper Raven Books
Printed in the United States of America
First Printing, 2022

ISBN= 978-1-7373195-3-5

Tom, thanks for always encouraging me and being a part of my crazy dreams…

~ CHAPTER 1 ~
THE HAPPY FAMILY

The gagging sound from the master bathroom stirred Curtis from his deep slumber.

"Are you okay, Kaylee? Do you need me to get you anything?"

"No, just give me a minute." Her weak voice was punctuated with retches and heaves.

He buried his head under the blankets in a futile attempt to avoid both the sounds coming from the mother of his unborn child, and the pungent aroma wafting into the bedroom.

"I love you, Kaylee. I'll run down to the kitchen and get you some crackers and ginger ale."

Curtis jumped out of bed and exited the room for the safety of the lower level. He bounded down the stairs, overjoyed at the reality that he finally had the family that he always dreamed of. He'd lost his parents as a teen and his grandparents in the last year, but he'd found Kaylee. The love of his life. His soulmate. And now there would be a child to complete their family unit.

Curtis hummed as he grabbed the bag of saltine crackers from the pantry and poured a glass of ginger ale to take to his love. He hoped this offering to the pregnancy gods would bring some refuge and the morning sickness would be short lived.

As he walked back into the bedroom, Kaylee reappeared from the bathroom, her face pale, blotting her mouth with the white towel as her hair fell in clumped strands around her face.

"You got a little something in your hair?" Curtis cautiously said with a slight shake in his voice.

"Damn!" She wiped her hair with the towel. "This puking better stop soon. I can't take this. I'm going to have to cut my hair off!"

"Oh no, babe, don't do that. We'll figure something out. I can hold your hair as you puke," Curtis offered. A smile crept across his face as he realized how crazy that sounded.

Kaylee lowered the towel, looking up through her lashes as she shook her head. "You never cease to amaze me."

"I'm so excited to be able to see our little baby's face today, even though it's on an ultrasound screen." Kaylee buckled the seat belt over her ever-growing belly, smiling as she thought of the precious cargo growing inside. "I remember when we first heard her heartbeat just a few months ago."

"Yes!" Curtis maneuvered the car down the driveway. "And hopefully we'll find out if she really is a girl. I know you think she is, but you never know. Maybe we are having a son."

"I know it's a girl, Curtis," Kaylee stated matter-of-factly. "Today the doctor will confirm it."

As they pulled into the parking lot of the doctor's office, Curtis wiped a trembling hand across his forehead. When they got out of the car, he reached for Kaylee's hand. She felt the cold sweat on his palm as their fingers intertwined. "Everything will be fine, Curtis. Our baby will be perfect, don't worry."

Smiling down at her, Curtis squeezed her hand. "I hope so."

Kaylee struggled with the impact he may have on their child. How would the child of a serial killer look? Would there be some sign of the monster they may become? Would a male child be more at risk than a female one?

Curtis knew she killed her abuser, but that wasn't the same. Since their paths had crossed in Winslow, Arizona, almost two years ago, this man had turned her world upside down. She would have to come clean to him soon, but not today. Today was about seeing their baby for the first time.

"Kaylee?" the nurse called as the door that led to the patient exam rooms opened.

"Yes." Kaylee stood and instinctively reached for Curtis's hand. This time it was warm, soft, and strong. As she rubbed her thumb over his fingers, they headed towards the nurse waiting at the door.

"We will be in room 220," the nurse said as they headed down the hall.

Curtis shook his head.

Kaylee remembered the connection to that number. It was the time he found his mother dead.

Why did it haunt him so? Why would the Universe never let him forget? She pushed the thoughts aside and focused on the excitement in the moment.

A few minutes later, Kaylee lay stretched out on the exam table in the darkened ultrasound room. All eyes were focused on the small screen with the blinking light. As the nurse expertly navigated the wand around Kaylee's belly, she pointed out specific measurements she was required to take of the femur, head, and the number of swallows the baby makes.

"Is this your first child?" she asked as they hung on to every word.

"Yes, it is," Kaylee responded.

"Do you want to know what the sex is?" the nurse asked.

"Absolutely!" Curtis said as he moved to the edge of his seat, almost falling out.

"Well, let's see if they will cooperate." She moved the wand around and snapped a few more pictures. "It's not a hundred percent, but it looks like you are having a beautiful little girl."

Kaylee and Curtis both let out a big sigh. "I knew she was a girl, Curtis!" Kaylee said confidently. "Our little Princess Stephanie, we love you already." She rubbed her hand across her baby bump.

As they walked through the parking lot hand in hand, the glow of meeting Stephanie lingered on their faces.

"I am so excited to meet our little girl." Curtis softly stroked Kaylee's back. "Family is so important, and I am so thankful that you have given me this gift."

Kaylee shuddered at the thought of expanding their family. What would this mean? Curtis had lost so much already. She didn't want to be the reason he lost his daughter too, but what if? The unknown troubled her. Could she save him? Could their love overcome his monster within? What about the monster within her? Time would tell, but could she spare the time? The thoughts of doubt raced through her head.

"A penny for your thoughts?" Curtis broke through her distraction.

"Oh Curtis, I'm sorry. I guess I am just feeling a little overwhelmed. This is all so much." She tried to convince herself as much as him while flipping through the ultrasound pictures the nurse printed. Running her finger over the profile of their daughter's face, her thoughts drifted back to that night in the park with Pappy.

As Kaylee had extended her hand to help Pappy climb over the rocks, he'd whispered, *Kaylee, I'm glad Curtis found you. He is very lucky, we both are. You are good for each other. I see a future for you two and for that I am glad. We are very blessed.*

The words rang loud in her head. She stroked her hand where his lips had gently kissed her. That was one of the last memories she had of Pappy before the fight that changed their path. No one saw that coming. What else didn't they see?

Curtis glanced over at her as they drove home in silence. With mouth pursed and brow furrowed, she lowered her eyes and stared at the outline of their baby's face. Her hand trembled as she traced it with her finger.

Kaylee knew the innocence of this child had them both confused. They would need to work together to protect her, to save her from the evils in the world. They needed to create a safe home for her. The plantation house at the farm would be that. The same place where Curtis had grown up, so would Stephanie. His mother had made it warm and welcoming, and she knew she and Curtis would carry that forward for Princess Stephanie as well. She had seen the vision in her dreams.

He reached over, placed his hand on Kaylee's thigh, and gave a supportive squeeze. She twitched. His hand provided warmth; energy moved between them, and she knew Curtis loved her and their baby, and would provide for them. That she did not worry about. He had money and a grand home. She had concerns about the emotional support, about the things she saw in her dreams.

"We will be okay, right?" She finally broke the silence.

"I think so, Kaylee." His voice was quiet but shaky. "We have never done this before. Neither of us. Let's face it, neither of us really had a model childhood. But I do know this—we love each other and we love this baby girl."

As her finger continued to outline the baby's profile, she said, "She has Pappy's nose."

"I think she will have a little bit of Pappy, Grandma, and Mom."

"Curtis," she paused as she lowered the picture and turned towards him. "Do you think we will be able to protect her?"

"We took down a raging lunatic serial killer in the desert; I think we can handle whatever is thrown at us, babe."

Kaylee laughed at the irony of that statement. "That's what I'm afraid of, Curtis. Do we even know what it is like to nurture and raise a person? A person that is one hundred percent reliant on us for everything. Do we have the skills to be able to instill the right values, morals? As you pointed out, neither of us have a proven track record in this area."

"You got me there. But we have four months to figure it out. Sometimes I really wish Mom and Pappy were still here. They would be a great help right now."

"We haven't killed Tucker, so we must be doing something right," Kaylee joked to lighten the mood. "But I'm not sure if you can compare taking care of Pappy's dog to taking care of a child."

"Ole Tuck is a little high maintenance for a hound, you know. So maybe there are some parallels." Curtis took her hand as they drove back to the plantation.

Tucker climbed off the wicker couch on the front porch. His tailed wagged as he stretched before bounding down the steps to greet them. Tucker had adjusted well to life with Curtis and Kaylee after Pappy died. He still preferred to wait on the front porch for them to return home, and he developed his daily rounds where he surveyed the farm as well as the house several times a day. One of the highlights of his day involved greeting the mailman. As soon as the sound of the mail truck reached his ears, he'd let out a loud, welcoming howl and trot down the drive wagging his tail.

As Curtis and Kaylee got out of the Mustang, Tucker let out his welcoming howl. They both grinned and patted him on the head. Taking care of a dog wasn't the same as taking care of a baby, but they both loved her and were determined to keep her safe.

———————•———————

In the darkness, Kaylee stirred. The pains were getting stronger, closer together. The due date was still a few weeks away, but the doctor said she may come early. She clenched her jaw as the contraction ripped through her womb. As she held her breath, fists clenched, she started to tremble.

Curtis rolled over and propped himself up on one elbow. "They are getting stronger." He reached for his watch to time the contractions. "That one was over a minute and they are almost five minutes apart."

"I think we should call the doctor. Stephanie wants to come out."

Curtis picked up the phone and dialed the number on the pad beside the bed. He spoke to the nurse and then hung up.

Kaylee looked at him as another wave of contractions ripped through her abdomen.

"They said the doctor will be calling us in a few minutes and to just keep track of the contractions." He jotted down the time and duration of the contractions on the pad of paper.

The phone rang a few minutes later. "Hello?" Curtis answered. "Kaylee, Dr. Silver wants to talk to you."

Kaylee fought to catch her breath before taking the phone. "They are getting stronger."

The reality of becoming a parent started to sink in. In a short time, she and Curtis would meet Princess Stephanie. Would Stephanie have her green eyes? Would she have strong hands like her dad or long, delicate fingers like her mom?

Dr. Silver's voice on the other end jolted her back into the present. "Kaylee? Kaylee? Are you okay? Are you still there?"

"Yes, yes, I'm still here. What did you ask?"

"Come to the hospital. I'm already here. I'll see you as soon as you get settled in your room."

Curtis was already out of bed and heading to the bathroom. They had planned this out. The bags were packed and by the door ready for Curtis to put them in the Mustang's trunk. When he came out of the bathroom, Kaylee was sitting on the edge of the bed.

"Are you okay? Can you get up?"

"Just give me a second." She pushed herself off the bed and Curtis helped her stand.

"Let's get you downstairs," he said as he guided her towards the door.

As they reached the bottom of the stairs, another contraction hit. Kaylee bent over and moaned as the pain shot around towards her back. "My back!" she screamed.

Curtis rubbed her lower back as they showed him during the birthing classes. It didn't seem to help. The contraction intensified. Finally, after several minutes, she straightened.

"That was a long one. We better get going or Stephanie is going to be a home birth."

Curtis helped her to the car, then ran back and grabbed the suitcases, hurling them into the trunk. The Mustang's engine roared to life and they sped down the drive.

Kaylee couldn't help but glance in the back seat to make sure the car seat was in place. Curtis had installed it the week before. *Car seat, check.*

Her dream was more vivid last night. It became clearer and clearer as the delivery day drew closer. She saw the death that followed Curtis. She struggled the last four months with when to tell Curtis. Now is not the time, not today.

~ CHAPTER 2 ~
AND BABY MAKES THREE

During the twenty-minute drive to Mercy General, Curtis struggled to keep the Mustang within the speed limit. With every contraction, he pushed the accelerator. Finally, they pulled into the parking lot. The large, blue labor and delivery sign blazed in the night sky. He maneuvered the car to the main door, jumped out, and ran around to help Kaylee. A nurse met them with a wheelchair.

"Hello, Mama," she said with a smile.

Kaylee smiled. "Thank God you have the chair. I don't think I can walk anymore."

"Let's get you inside and checked in," the nurse said as she got Kaylee into the wheelchair. "What's your name, love? And who's your doctor?"

"Kaylee Smith-Roberts and Dr. Silver is my doctor."

"Very well. I think I saw your name on the list. Dr. Silver just told us to expect you." She pushed the chair through the automatic doors into the hospital birthing center lobby.

"Dad," she said as she looked at Curtis, "why don't you go get Kaylee checked in and I'll take her back to her room so we can see when this little nugget is planning on making a debut."

Curtis nodded as he walked over to the check-in desk. The patient registration sign marked the cubicle where he pulled out the rust-colored chair and sat down. An older lady dressed in scrubs with little bunnies greeted him with a warm smile.

"Let's get you guys checked in, shall we?"

Curtis simply nodded. His mind spun wildly. The self-doubt he carried with him for so long weighed heavy. He thought of his mom. She always gave him strength, told him everything was okay, that he was okay. Suddenly, he heard Kaylee's voice in his head, *I am here for you, always.* The abruptness startled him and he must have twitched as it caused the nurse to look up.

"Everything all right?"

"Yes. This is all a little overwhelming." He wondered if he would ever get used to Kaylee's mind communication.

"We get that a lot with first-time parents. It will be fine," she said in a soothing tone. "You both will make awesome parents. Now, what is the mom's name?"

Curtis answered her questions for what seemed like hours. The speed of his thoughts caused him to lose track of time. In reality, it was only about fifteen minutes. Finally, the nurse gave him a bracelet to wear.

"She is in room 220. The elevators are straight back to the left."

Curtis pushed the chair back.

"Is everything okay, Mr. MacIntyre?" The registration nurse had a bewildered look on her face.

Curtis again nodded as he slowly got up and turned towards the elevators. He shook his head as he tried in vain to remove the words he had just heard. He got to the elevator, pushed the button, and waited for its arrival. The numbers above the dark arrows clicked down, six, five, four…. The countdown to his destiny. He watched the elevator draw closer. Hopefully, it is the start of a new beginning and not the beginning of the end. The bell signaled his need to step aboard for the ride of his life.

The doors opened to the second floor, and Curtis hesitated a moment when the doors started to close. He stuck his foot out to reverse them before he stepped across the threshold into the bustling hallway of the maternity ward. He looked both ways, bewildered by which way to go when he heard a cheerful voice.

"What room are you looking for?"

Curtis turned around to see a tall, slender nurse in pink scrubs with a colorful, short scarf tied around her neck. He stared at her and the scarf as evil thoughts raced through his mind. His silence lasted too long.

"Sir? Are you looking for a specific room?" the nurse asked again as she reached out and touched his arm.

His eyes followed her hand. Instinctively, he reached up and laid his hand over hers, shook his head, and answered, "Yes. I'm sorry. I'm a little out of it. I'm looking for Kaylee Smith-Roberts in room 220."

"That room is right down here at the end of the hall. I'll take you there." She placed her second hand over his and gave it a slight squeeze.

There was something about her. Their paths had crossed before. He smiled and tilted his head. She raised her eyebrow the same way he does. Did she recognize him too? They stared in each other's eyes, both silent. Why was she toying with me? He hesitantly broke her stare, smiled at her, and laughed.

"We best get going. I'm sure Kaylee is wondering where her baby's daddy is."

"Of course, sir."

"My name is Curtis."

"Hi, Curtis." A big smile crossed her face as she reached up and twirled the ends of her scarf. "I volunteer here, so I'll try to stop in and check on you."

"That would be nice." Curtis and the volunteer walked towards the end of the hall. "It's nice that you volunteer at the hospital."

"It's not as noble as it seems. I got in a little trouble, so I have some community service hours to work off. I did get to pick the place, and a hospital seemed like a good option."

"I see. Well, I'm glad you picked this hospital."

She was familiar. They had crossed paths on his travels just before he met Kaylee. Did she remember him? Did she want him to remember her?

"Here we are, Curtis." She motioned to the room with 220 on the sign.

"Thank you." Curtis furrowed his brow. "I'm sorry, I don't believe you told me your name?"

"Kristi."

"Kristi," Curtis repeated. "With a *K* and two *I*'s."

Kristi laughed. "You remembered."

"Some people you never forget."

Her face took on a pink hue.

He winked and bowed towards her and waved his arm.

"Thanks, my lady, for taking pity on me and helping me find my way."

"You are most welcome, kind sir." She pulled out her pretend skirt and curtsied before she turned away.

"Curtis? Is that you?" Kaylee's voice beckoned from inside the room.

"Yes, Kaylee. I needed a little help finding the room." He turned abruptly and walked through the doorway.

The room was cold, clinical, and unwelcoming. The walls were lined with machines, computers, and rolling carts filled with medical supplies. There was a chair in the corner by the window that was for the dad to sleep in so he could stay in the hospital. Curtis eyed the uncomfortable-looking chair. He knew he needed to stay with Kaylee and Princess Stephanie, but he dreaded sleeping there. She would be born early, but hopefully, she'd come home in the standard two to three days.

Kaylee was hooked up to monitors, wires were everywhere, and the IV was already in her arm. A nurse bustled around the room as she checked the monitors, adjusted the IV drips, and organized the wires.

"My name's Sandy. I'll be your nurse. Everything is going well." Walking to the board near the door, she wrote her name and some notes. "You are five centimeters, so it may be a little bit. But with first-time labors, you never know. It can go very quickly."

She glanced over at Curtis before returning her attention to Kaylee. "Do you want me to bring you anything? Some ice water perhaps?"

"That would be great!" Kaylee responded as she adjusted herself on the bed. Her eyes scrunched up.

"Another contraction?" Curtis reached over and took her hand while he stroked her hair with the other.

Kaylee nodded as she bit her lip.

Sandy pointed to the bottom monitor. "This line shows the contractions. The height shows the intensity. They will get double that." She continued to point out the other numbers on the screens. "This is the baby's heart rate and this is Mom's."

"Princess Stephanie has a fast, strong heartbeat." Curtis stared at the various numbers and lines flashing on the screen.

"Yes, she does. Babies' hearts beat much faster than ours." Sandy glanced at Kaylee's face squished in pain. "Kaylee, are you okay? Do you want me to call the anesthesiologist?"

Kaylee nodded her head as she held her breath.

Curtis watched the line showing the contractions as it climbed higher. It peaked and started its downward trek.

"I will call them now. It may be a few minutes before they get here, so try to rest in between."

"Thanks, Sandy." Curtis focused on Kaylee, but his thoughts drifted back to Kristi. He never forgot a face.

◆——●——◆

As she let go of the illusion that it could be any different, Kristi placed her hand on her stomach. The life that had come from her over a year ago was all the motivation she needed. She was excited for the future. She didn't expect to see him. Not here. Not ever.

Kristi reflected on the journey that took her to this point. She never thought the night at the truck stop back in Tennessee would turn out how it did. Their daughter was a year old and here he was with another pregnant mother getting ready to give birth. This child was Genevieve's sibling. But he could never know.

She knew he recognized her. She could tell not just from the way he looked at her, but his comment about the *K* and two *I*s. Torn between wanting to rush into his arms and remain a distant memory, she struggled with what to do next. She was fine on her own. She went through the pregnancy without him. She had been raising their daughter alone. They had a place to live, food on the table; they didn't want for anything. She didn't need nor want any additional drama in her life. He must never know.

If she could go back to the day they met, would she turn around and walk away? Things would be drastically different. He hadn't crossed her mind for months. At first, it was hard. She thought of him often. Then she figured things out and built a life for her and her daughter. Her blonde hair reminded her of Curtis. The curls were from Kristi's side of the family.

From birth, Genevieve had striking eyes. They were always blue, but as she got older something changed. They started getting yellow streaks in them. Bright yellow circles enclosed her pupils and radiated out through the deep blue irises. She had never seen anything like it. Enchanting and mesmerizing, she had the ability to hypnotize you simply by pulling you in with her eyes.

Kristi had asked the doctor if something was wrong. They explained Genevieve had a rare condition referred to as central heterochromia, where the outer ring of ones iris is a different color from the rest. Most likely genetic. When she looked at Genevieve's eyes, it was a constant reminder that the blood that coursed through her veins was not entirely hers. It was from someone that neither of them knew. A mysterious donor that she had hoped would remain unknown.

When she saw him at the elevator, something drew her in. As she looked in his eyes, she saw it. The blue color with just a hint of pale yellow. It wasn't as striking as Genevieve's but was detectable if you were looking. She needed to stay away. Nothing good would come from continued contact.

As she went about her duties, she found herself finding reasons not only to be in the maternity ward, but to walk past room 220. It was inevitable their paths would cross again.

The next morning, she arrived at the front desk greeted by a wonderful bouquet of flowers. The vase was stunning. A prism of light radiated from the cuts in the glass as the sun passed through.

"Those are gorgeous!" she exclaimed as she spun them around. "Look at that vase."

"They just arrived. Destined for the maternity ward." The guard picked up a large pink teddy bear. "This goes with it."

"Room 220, Kaylee Smith-Roberts," Kristi read on the tag. "I'm headed that way. I'll just drop them off."

"Perfect. Saves me from calling someone else."

Kristi picked up the flowers and the large bear and headed towards the elevator. She knew she would see him. Maybe one day his name wouldn't make her smile, but that wasn't today.

As she exited the elevator and turned towards the room, she felt butterflies in her stomach. Her pace slowed as she approached the room. She paused outside the door, composed herself, took a deep breath, and headed in.

"Good morning." She set the flowers on the bedside table. "These just arrived for you."

"They are beautiful." Kaylee reached for the card. "Oh Curtis, thank you so much."

Kristi looked over at Curtis still lying uncomfortably in the reclining chair.

"Those aren't the most pleasing accommodations, are they?" She laughed as she watched him struggle to get out of the confines of the chair that imprisoned him.

"Certainly not! And not very easy to escape from either." He stretched as the bones in his back cracked. "I would probably feel better if I slept on the floor."

"Oh, Curtis," Kaylee said as she swaddled little Stephanie in her arms and showed her the bear. "It's not that bad."

"You slept in the bed!" They bantered back and forth.

"Enjoy your time with your new daughter," Kristi said as she turned to leave.

"Can you show me the way to the cafeteria?" Curtis finally escaped the confines of the recliner.

"Sure." Kristi looked back over her shoulder. "I was just headed down there myself."

"Maybe you could keep Curtis company?" Kaylee asked. "I really could use some quiet time. Stephanie was up several times last night and it looks like she is ready for a nap."

"New babies have their own schedule." Kristi smiled at Curtis. "Ready?"

"Always." He kissed Kaylee and Stephanie on their heads and followed Kristi out to the hallway.

Kristi and Curtis enjoyed a delicious breakfast in the hospital cafeteria.

"Nice first date." He finished the last of his coffee. "Normally, I would choose a little nicer place."

"Like a truck stop?" she said, a hint of sarcasm in her voice.

"Again, not my best choice."

"You look good." He refilled his cup and topped hers off. "You have any kids?"

"Kids?" She paused for a moment as she contemplated her next move. "No, no kids for me."

Would he see the guilt in her eyes? Why would he? He had no reason to think he was the father of any other children.

"Too bad." He brought the hot liquid to his lips. "You would make a great mother. You have a way with people."

A big smile came upon her face as she flipped her hair to the side. Oh how she wished he knew.

~ CHAPTER 3 ~

DREAMS BECOME REALITY

Curtis and Kaylee snuggled with their new baby daughter, Princess Stephanie. She had steel blue-gray eyes, a head of dark brown hair, dramatic eyelashes, and plump red lips. As she peered down at the angelic face, Kaylee wondered if her eyes would change to green like hers or stay blue like Curtis's.

There are moments that mark your life. Moments you realize nothing will ever be the same again. These moments divide time into two parts, before this and after this. Stephanie's birth was one of those defining moments for them both.

The last few days had been a blur. The hours of pushing, the emotional and physical exhaustion she felt coupled with exhilaration of bringing a new life into this world had taken its toll. Her eyes felt heavy as she drifted off to sleep with Stephanie lying on her chest wrapped tightly in her blanket.

As her subconscious swirled trying to make sense of her future, vivid dreams began to take shape. Out of a cloud of purple, a figure appeared. She couldn't quite make them out, but she could hear their message: "Take care of my family. Trust in his love. He will protect you both. Do not let what you know scare you. Be strong." Kaylee could hear the words as they hung in the air and circled around in the purple fog. The figure moved towards something surrounded by a bright light. It was so bright Kaylee couldn't make out what it was no matter how much she strained her eyes. The purple fog swirled and stung them. Her hand instinctively shielded her face from the strange-colored haze. A strong pungent odor wafted into her nose. It was foul and vile, like the unholy putrefaction of a thousand corpses. The smell was so powerful it made her gag in her sleep. She recognized the smell of death. Once experienced, it was something you never forgot. But why? What was the message it brought?

Kaylee started to move closer to the bright light. Her eyes turned to slits in defense of the intensity.

The fog started to thin. She looked down into a deep pit in the ground. It was filled with bodies of women and men. They were dressed in clothes, some from decades before, some more modern. She noticed one woman with a red, white, and blue scarf tied around her neck. The smell intensified as she stood above the mass grave.

A man she didn't recognize spoke. "These are the Masons' doing."

People kept coming, carrying bodies and placing them on the pile. A woman laid her sacred cargo down, turned, and faced Kaylee.

Her eyes narrowed. "You are late."

"Late for what? I didn't do this. This isn't my fault."

Other voices joined in. "You are late. You are late."

The chatting grew louder and louder. Kaylee covered her ears.

"STOP!!!"

The light flashed, followed by complete darkness. Kaylee could tell she was no longer in the field; she felt cold stone under her bare feet. Her eyes adjusted and she realized she was in a cave with bars.

Stephanie was with her and they were both covered in blood.

She awoke covered in sweat. Kaylee heard her quickened pulse as it pounded in her ears. She struggled to understand the message in her dream. She still tasted the smell of death in her mouth. How did it relate to the other dreams? Who was the messenger? Why was she late? Was this simply the hormone surge during labor, or was it something more?

◆————————•————————◆

Ever since she was a little girl, Kaylee saw the future in her dreams. She had seen Curtis's face before she met him in Winslow, Arizona. In the past, the visions were stories of the future, but since she got pregnant they had changed to warnings shrouded in secrecy, distorted by fog and bright lights. She must confide in Curtis. She needed to tell him what lay ahead. She wanted to confirm these premonitions first.

She quickly picked up her phone and dialed the familiar number. The warm voice answered, "Good morning. I often wonder why you choose to use technology instead of telepathy for our communications."

"Habit, I guess," Kaylee chuckled. "Abigail, I am in need of serious guidance and direction."

Kaylee first met Abigail when she was a teenager. Her friends had decided to go visit a palm reader and psychic one Friday night. She did not expect much and was shocked at the accuracy of the reading and the insight that Abigail conveyed. Although they both possessed telepathic abilities, Abigail's talents were far more advanced than Kaylee's at the time.

For as long as she could remember, Kaylee knew people's thoughts and emotions before they spoke. Her mom always said this was because she was a sensitive child, but not until she met Abigail did she truly understand the gift she possessed. Upon their first meeting, Abigail cautiously explained she could see the future. She could also feel and experience other's thoughts and memories. She went on to say that Kaylee had suffered a lot of pain and despair in her short life, but that her actions had alleviated a major source. Kaylee immediately knew she was referring to her stepfather.

Abigail read her mind and simply stated, "Christopher can't hurt you anymore. You made sure of that."

Kaylee recoiled at the sound of his name. "How do you…?" Her voice trailed off.

Before she finished, she heard in her head Abigail's voice. "*You brought his name forward in your thoughts. I simply received it. You have the same ability should you want to develop it.*"

Kaylee tried in vain to clear her mind of all thoughts. "What else do you see?"

"You have a bright, impactful future. You will spend your life helping others find their way. You will meet your soulmate and recognize him instantly."

Their conversation went on for an hour before Abigail ended it.

"Our journey together has just begun. Our path is long. Until next time, be well, my friend."

Kaylee sat motionless as she digested what she had been told. Her thoughts raced, jumped from one thing to the next, as she tried to make sense of it.

"*Be still, young one. All will become clear.*" Abigail's soft, calm voice entered her thoughts.

Kaylee smiled and nodded as Abigail squeezed her hands.

"I think it's time for me to move onto your friends."

Kaylee cleared her mind and focused on the present as Abigail explained the message in her dreams. She explained the cave was a sign, a representation of that she felt trapped and wanted to leave but something was holding her back. Stephanie was with her not because she was in danger, but rather to signify that that was what was holding her back.

She conveyed that Kaylee was not alone. Divine spirits helped her overcome the earthly obstacles she encountered. She mentioned the angel number 220 for the first time.

"Why would you bring that up?" her voice trembled as she awaited the reply.

"This number is very telling; it has surrounded you and Curtis. The number two represents duty, relationships, and life purpose. When doubled, the aspects are stronger and very dominant. The number two is a symbol of pairs; twenty-two conveys stable relationships in all aspects: romantic, love, family, life."

That sounded positive and brought Kaylee a sense of relief.

"Don't conclude too fast, my dear," Abigail warned as she read her thoughts. "This number also represents great fear. Fear of losing people, of being alone, or," she paused a bit before continuing, "fear of dependency."

Dependency. Why did that elicit such a visceral response?

"You have always struggled to be in control. From a young child, you have been dominated by men in your life. The number zero is intriguing. Being extremely strong spiritually, it is a symbol of eternity, a circle of overall life, the celestial vibration," Abigail explained. "The number 220 is very powerful and inspiring but if not handled correctly, it can be damaging and lethal. It has the potential to create and destroy."

"So that's why that number haunts Curtis so. Is it only around me and Stephanie because of Curtis?"

"That, dear, I cannot say for sure. You have a strong personality and you have goals you want to achieve, but try not to hurt others along the way. I see much pain in your future with Curtis. Problems are not always best solved by direct action. Focus on going through the stories in your head. Separate truth from fears, reality from perception."

Kaylee hesitated to bring it up. She wondered if Abigail knew.

"During the last dream, there was a smell."

"The scent of death. I wondered if you wanted to know about that. One smells death when something has changed or needs to change. It is no longer of value to you and you need to let it go. It can be a reflection of the past. You tend to dwell on what you know. You need to move forward and leave your past behind."

"Thank you for the clarity and insight. I have a lot to think about."

"Go in peace and may your thoughts still," Kaylee heard in her mind as the phone went dead.

As she walked over to the bassinet and picked up Stephanie, she looked down at her angelic face. "Princess Stephanie, I will always protect you before all others, that I promise. We will follow our path. I will choose wisely for both of us. There will be no regrets." She walked down the stairs and found Curtis as he cooked breakfast.

"Good morning, sleepyheads." He spooned the eggs onto plates and added bacon strips to the side. "I thought you could use some extra sleep as you were stirring a lot last night."

"Not the best night's sleep. Maybe it's the hormones." She sat at the table, cradling Stephanie in her lap. "That looks good. I'm starving," she said, wanting to redirect the conversation.

While tasting the eggs, a memory of childhood snuck into her mind. "I can remember growing up and Mom cooking a big breakfast on weekends. Eggs, bacon, pancakes. Those were some great times. Before it all went to shit."

Curtis tilted his head and asked, "It can be good again, right?"

"I won't let it be anything else for this precious angel." She gazed at sleeping Stephanie in her lap with her head snuggled in her bent knee.

Curtis walked around the table and placed his hand on her shoulder. "We got this. I will protect you both, always."

A shiver shot through Kaylee's body, Stephanie stirred, and Curtis jerked back his hand.

"What did I say?"

"Nothing. It's just I've been having a weird dream for a while and someone is telling me that your love will protect us and not to worry."

"That sounds like good advice to me." He smiled and kissed her head. "Let's finish up the eggs and we can take our princess out for some sunshine. I do have to run out tonight to take care of some business."

Kaylee nodded. She knew what that meant. Curtis needed to feed his thirst for death. What triggered that drive baffled her. She reflected on Abigail's words. "Separate truth from fears, reality from perception. Problems are not always solved by direct action." She knew the vision was real and spoke the truth. The message from the shadowed figure may have been her mind's way of accepting her fate. But the cave signified that she felt trapped and wanted to leave. The bars were the signal that she shouldn't leave now. Stephanie was barely a month old. She needed more time, months maybe years. She knew she couldn't rip Stephanie from her father now. She learned to be content with no action.

As she began to accept this decision over the coming weeks, Abigail's voice entered her thoughts. *"Continue to take care of yourself. You are where you are meant to be. Leave the past behind. Relax and truly feel what it's like to let go of your fears. Things will become much easier to you."*

Weeks turned to months, and her heart warmed as she exhaled deeply and released all the negative energy to the Universe. Her fears, her doubts. As she breathed in peace and harmony, she laughed. Harmony and serial killer was ironic, but she was at peace with her decision.

~ CHAPTER 4 ~
LIKE AN OLD PAIR OF BOOTS

"Come on, Tuck!" Curtis called to the dog as he gathered his supplies in a backpack and headed to the Mustang parked in the driveway.

The last rays of the day cast their glow across the sky as he and Tucker got in the car. The excitement grew in the pit of his stomach as he placed the backpack within easy reach of the driver's seat. He felt like a kid at Christmas. He hadn't been hunting for several months, but some things you never forget. He pulled down the visor and opened the mirror.

"Looking good," he said to Tucker as he inspected his reflection. "Should be an easy one."

Curtis had scouted a lady that worked nights at a convenience store in a town about an hour away. He thought that bringing Tucker along would make him less threatening. This wasn't normal routine but for some reason, a change of pace seemed in order.

He glanced at his watch. "A little over three hours before she takes her dinner break. Just enough time to swing by the jeweler on the way." Curtis maneuvered the car down the driveway while Tucker rode shotgun.

Curtis parked the car in front of Johnson's Jewelers. "Well, boy, time to go make this official." He patted Tucker on the head as he got out of the car and headed into the store.

The color in the western sky started to appear. He paused to admire nature's beauty. Mama always preferred sunrise to sunset. The start of a new beginning. She always reminded him to leave the past where it belongs and to begin again in a new way. Each sunrise was a constant reminder of his mother's philosophy that lived on in him. He would make sure he passed that on to Stephanie as well.

A butterfly danced towards him, fluttering about. It landed on his shirt. As he looked down at it, he knew it was her by the lavender in its stained-glass wings. Before she passed on, Curtis asked her for a symbol so he knew she was there. It was a purple butterfly. She was always with him, always and forever.

Curtis glanced through the case filled with diamond engagement rings. Kaylee was the one for him and with Stephanie's first birthday coming up, this was the time to commit.

"I'm looking for something unique, teardrop-shaped, with lots of sparkle," Curtis explained to the man behind the counter.

He looked over the rings that the salesman chose and placed on the velvet-covered board for his inspection. The large, pear-shaped solitaire with sleek, baguette-cut diamonds on either side set in bright platinum caught his eye. The stone reminded him of a blood drop. It was symmetrical. The point was created as it fought to part from its owner, until finally, gravity pulled the weight of the blood severing the connection. He hoped the connection between him and Kaylee would never be severed; his logical nature conveyed a different reality. For now, Kaylee was content with him and allowing him to be a part of Stephanie's life.

"I think this is the one." Curtis held the ring and rocked it between his fingers. The diamonds sparkled brilliantly as rainbows of colors radiated into the air. "Yes, this is Kaylee's ring. The perfect mix of me and her."

"Nice choice, sir." The salesman shined the ring and placed it in the box.

Curtis paid for the ring and slipped it into his pocket as he exited the store and headed back to the car where Tucker waited.

"Got the ring, Tuck. Now on to the next errand."

He took the box from his pocket, opened the glove box, and paused as he saw the stack of scarves neatly ordered in the compartment. He set the ring inside as he took the top scarf off the pile.

"This one will do nicely." He shoved it into his pocket that housed Kaylee's ring just a few moments ago.

As the ninth hour grew near, Curtis approached the Hop & Stop convenience store. He looked through the front windows. She headed back to the storeroom to take her break. "Timed this perfectly." He snapped the leash onto Tucker's collar. "Come on, ole boy, let's go charm our next victim."

Tucker and Curtis headed across the parking lot to the grassy knoll at the back of the store. As they walked through the grass, she came out the back door and headed over to sit on the hill a few hundred feet from them. Tucker raised his head and watched her. His nose twitched as she unwrapped her hot sandwich. Tucker pulled on the leash as he headed toward the lady. Saliva started to drip from his mouth in anticipation that she would offer him a bite of her meal.

As they got closer, Curtis corrected him. "Tucker, she doesn't want to share her dinner with you."

The woman glanced over; her gaze lit with appreciation. Women seemed to appreciate his casual T-shirt-and-jeans look, and enough of them had commented on his good looks and muscles. He was happy to use that to his advantage.

"Hi, Tucker. Aren't you a pretty boy?" She reached out a hand to pet his head.

Tucker sat down in the grass and wagged his tail.

"Sorry, ma'am. Tucker seems to have forgotten his manners."

"No worries. I would enjoy the company."

"We were just passing through town and stopped to stretch our legs a bit." Curtis sat on the grass with Tucker between them.

"I'm on my break. Just enjoying the cool night air." She finished her sandwich. "It's been a slow night. Not a lot of customers, so I've been stocking the shelves. It feels good to sit and relax."

They enjoyed pleasant banter as she finished her sandwich.

Curtis stretched his arms over his head. "I'm getting too old for these long drives. My back starts to ache after just a few hours."

"Do you want to walk around a bit? There's a nice trail right over there." She motioned towards the park behind them.

He glanced towards the park. "Sounds good. I'm sure Tucker would love to run around a bit too. Do you think anyone would care if I let him off his leash?"

"Not this time of night. It's pretty quiet." She stood and headed over towards the trail.

"Come on, ole boy." He unclipped the leash from Tucker's collar. The hound shook his head and trotted off after the lady as his tail wagged behind him.

"Seems he prefers you." Curtis laughed as he jogged to catch up with them.

"The stars are pretty bright tonight." She reached down and scratched Tucker behind his ear as he trotted passed.

They walked down the path. Right on cue, Tucker spied a squirrel. He put his head down, paused just a second before he let out a mighty howl, and off he went after the rodent. He zigged and zagged back and forth as he tried endlessly to catch the little creature before the squirrel ran for the cover of the woods.

"Tucker! Tucker, come!" Curtis called fruitlessly as he watched his hound disappear into the dark woods. The edge of his lips curled up slightly as he added, "Well, guess that wasn't a good idea."

"I'll help you find him. I'm sure he didn't go very far." She headed off towards the woods calling for his dog.

Curtis slipped his hand inside his pocket and felt the silky fabric neatly folded inside. As they got closer to the woods, the darkness engulfed everything. The moonlight filtered through the branches and the leaves rustled in the light breeze, creating a sinister ambience. He saw Tucker with his feet resting on a tree truck as he looked up into the branches.

"Looks like the squirrel got away from you, Tuck," Curtis called out to his dog as they got closer.

"Poor buddy. All that chasing and no prize," she said as Curtis grabbed Tucker's collar and gave him a hearty pat on his side.

They started to walk back towards the edge of the woods. He needed to act now while the trees offered some protection for potential passersby. He looked around. She was right when she said no one used the park this time of night.

Curtis pulled the scarf from his pocket and wrapped it around his hands. As he stepped up behind her, he raised his arms as he slipped the scarf over her head and pulled it tight around her neck. He crossed his hands behind her head as she reached up and clawed at the fabric in vain.

Tucker sat down beside the tree and glanced between his master and the squirrel high in the tree branches.

As she struggled, Curtis turned her around and looked in her eyes. Tears welled up in them and started to fall down her cheeks. He tipped his head to the side and hesitated a second before he grabbed her neck with his hands. As he dug his fingers into her flesh, he thought of the innocence of his daughter. How he would never let anyone hurt her the way that these women had been hurt. Although Curtis rarely spoke to his victims as he killed them, he felt an urge this time.

"I will set you free. You will no longer be fearful to go home to that man. He will never hurt you again. I will save you." His grip tightened around her neck.

The confused look in her eyes made Curtis continue. "You may not understand now. But you will. I set women free. I save them from the heartache and bad memories they experience. I will set you free!"

He watched as the red dots appeared in her eyes and her hands went limp along with her body. He set her on the ground as Tucker sniffed her lifeless body. He walked a few yards away to where he had stashed a backpack with a large tarp in it. He wrapped her up and threw her over his shoulder as he walked out of the woods to where he had parked the Mustang. He placed her in the trunk. He and Tucker jumped back in the car and the engine roared to life as he drove out of the dark parking lot, heading back to the farm.

As the meat grinder in the old shed roared to life, he dropped the pieces of her dismembered body into the chute. His thoughts drifted to Kaylee and Stephanie. It had been almost a year since they brought that angel home from the hospital and things between him and Kaylee had never been better.

He wiped the blood from his hand, reached into his pocket, and retrieved the small box. As he opened it, he thought of the permanency it represented. It exemplified both of them. Her sparkling brilliance and his thirst for blood. They were different, almost opposites, yet somehow they seamlessly complemented each other. The Universe had brought them together at the right time in their separate journeys to create the family they both dreamt of.

A smile grew across his face as he snapped the box shut. He knew the perfect spot and the perfect time.

~ CHAPTER 5 ~
THE PROPOSAL

The morning sun peeked into the bedroom, casting dancing shapes of light across the wood floor. Curtis had been up for hours. He planned this day for weeks and thought about it for months. He finished making breakfast, setting the plate filled with waffles and strawberries beside the glass of juice on the silver tray. Stephanie would be getting up soon, so time was of the essence. He put the vase containing three roses, a red one, a white one, and a lavender one onto the tray. As he looked over his masterpiece, he smiled. This was the moment he would finally have a family of his own.

As he neared the bedroom doorway, he heard Stephanie crying and Kaylee's voice as she tried to settle her.

"Sweet baby, let's just get this diaper changed and we'll get something to eat."

As Curtis walked into the room and set the tray on the table between the two chairs, the sunbeam landed right on the vase of roses.

"Look what Daddy brought us, Steph." Kaylee patted Stephanie's back and she quieted. "To what do we owe this unexpected treat?"

"I just wanted to spoil you."

Kaylee smiled and kissed Curtis before bending to smell the roses. «They smell so good. Did you cut them from the garden?"

"I did. The red one for love. The lavender one as it represents love at first sight and enchantment. The white is for innocence."

"You are just full of surprises." She sat in the chair, settling Stephanie in her lap. "Every time I think I have you figured out, you do something to throw me for a loop." She took a big bite of the waffle and fruit. "These strawberries are amazing. So sweet."

"I knew you would enjoy them." His chest puffed out almost involuntarily as he boasted.

Stephanie grabbed a strawberry covered in whipped cream. The cream covered her face as she devoured the sweet treat.

«I thought we could spend the day at the beach. I think we can all use a fun day in the surf and sand."

"That sounds perfect. I just got Steph a cute new swimsuit, and since she is just starting to walk, she'll really love playing in the water and building castles."

"You two finish up that yummy breakfast I slaved over, and I'll put together a bag for us." He turned with a lightness in his step. Things were finally going to work out.

As the girls finished eating, Curtis rounded up the essentials for a day at the beach. The drive was only a few hours, so they wouldn't need much for the ride. After he put the cooler, beach chairs, and bag into the truck, he reached into his pocket and pulled out the small velvet box. As he placed it into the glove box, he thought how much was riding on the contents of that small box. His entire future rested in her hands. He knew she was hesitant about raising Stephanie with a serial killer. But he had it under control. Who better to protect her if something did go wrong than the most prolific serial killer? He inhaled deeply, expanding his chest as Kaylee approached the car. This was going to be a great day.

———•———

They spent the day jumping over the waves and digging in the sand. Curtis helped build deep moats around Stephanie's sand towers as they tried in vain to control the unforgiving water. The foaming salt water rushed in and filled up the trench he expertly constructed, only to saturate the very foundation on which they built. Stephanie laughed as she built castle after castle only to have them washed away without a trace by the relentless surf.

Kaylee watched them build their mighty kingdom again and again, only to have it melt away. She was glad that Stephanie found humor in this irony, as she did not. She knew the life she was building with Curtis did not offer stability. The foundation was built on quicksand. When it implodes, it would pull everything in its path to its doom.

As her daughter and the man she loved played carelessly in the bright sun, her thoughts drifted to the message in her dreams. The image of the figure cloaked in the purple fog. The voice that told her she needed to trust him, to not be scared of what she knew. He would protect her. It was a sharp contrast to the pit with countless bodies and a trail of people as they walked to lay more on the pile. Could she truly accept Curtis and all his baggage?

She reflected on the dream and Abigail's wisdom. Kaylee sensed there were more warnings to come. The spirits loomed in the background, silently waiting, watching, judging. She was truly late to the party, in so many ways.

Lying back in the warm sand, she closed her eyes. Vivid hues of red, purple, and blue swirled inside her eyelids from the bright sun. Abigail's voice entered her mind.

"The time for clearing your soul is near. Your truth must be told. An important decision requires it."

Kaylee kept her eyes shut as she reflected on the message and the fear of what may come drifted across her body. Her fists clenched as she felt her heart start to pound in her chest and her breathing quickened. Could she confess not only the vision of his future but also what she was doing in Flagstaff two years ago when they first met? Kaylee had written the article. She was able to link him to over thirty missing women, but she was certain there were more.

After they had killed the Serpent, they flawlessly executed the story she wove to protect Curtis. The thirty-five murders assigned to Henry Blackwell, the Serpent, were not all his doing. Kaylee had offered some of her notes to the detectives. As he had tracked Curtis, their paths overlapped for quite some time. Because he was deceased, the investigation was not very robust. Some of the missing people dated back a decade, which made the local detectives more than eager to close these longstanding cases on the weakest of evidence.

Abigail's voice once again echoed through her mind. *"Separate truth from fears. Live your truth, the one that is in your heart."*

Kaylee opened her eyes. She knew this was the day she would tell him. She was at peace with her decision. Something stilled nagged at her. There was another question that she would face soon. This one would not prove as easy.

The sun moved closer to the horizon as the water's edge approached their blanket. As the tide rolled in, the sandcastles gave way to a lagoon Curtis dug to cool them off. Small crawdads scurried about as the waves refilled their pool. Stephanie tried to catch them, but they burrowed into the sand, reemerging with each wave, swimming furiously in the warm salt water. As the beach emptied of its visitors, Kaylee sensed Curtis growing restless.

"Are you okay?" She knew what the answer would be.

"I'm fine." He got up and rifled through the bag containing suntan lotion, snacks, and the small velvet box hidden in the zippered compartment.

Kaylee looked out at the horizon as the sky darkened and the air started to noticeably cool. She focused on the sound from the waves and barely noticed Curtis as he knelt beside her.

"Kaylee." His voice soft and reassuring. "A lot has happened over the past two years and through it all you have been my rock."

Kaylee turned and saw him with the closed box in his hand and her eyes filled with tears. This was the moment she had longed for and dreaded at the same time. She knew she loved him. She knew he was the man she was supposed to be with. Her soulmate. Yet she also knew his secret. She was his accomplice by omission. As tears started to run down her cheek, Stephanie climbed out of the sand pool and wrapped her arm around her mother's neck.

Curtis continued, "You have given me the greatest gifts in life, your love and our little Princess Stephanie."

Stephanie giggled as she squeezed Kaylee's neck.

As he opened the box, the last rays of the sun reflected off the near perfect stone and the sparkle blinded them. "Kaylee, will you do me the honor of spending the rest of your life with me and be my wife?"

The sparkly ring was too much for Stephanie to resist as she reached towards the box. "Not so fast, sweetheart; Mommy hasn't said yes." Kaylee pulled their daughter back to her lap. "I love you with all that I am. I've seen you without your mask, but you haven't seen behind mine. It's only fair that we both lay everything out in the open. We both need to stand naked with all our scars and truths exposed."

Curtis sat in the sand at her feet and placed his hand on her knee. "Nothing you say will change my mind."

"Maybe not, but I still need to tell you." Kaylee started at the beginning back in Chicago with Sarah and what brought her to Flagstaff that spring. "I was researching a story about missing women along Route 40. I had figured out the scarf link and had created a pretty strong profile." She paused as she gauged Curtis's reaction.

"What makes me a great investigator is that I don't truly work alone. The visions I see in my dreams foreshadow things to come. I saw your face before we met. I knew you were the one that I was looking for. I just didn't know it was my heart that was searching." Stephanie wiggled in her lap as she searched for a more comfortable spot. "We both have killed, but for very different reasons and at a much different frequency. When you first took me to the plantation house, I searched at night for the trophies you kept from your victims."

"Did you find them?"

"I did." She shook her head as the disbelief still shocked her. "The sheer number was startling. There must have been one hundred of them."

"Seventy-five at that time," Curtis boasted. "Seventy-six actually, but I hadn't added the scarf I collected in Arizona the morning after we met in Winslow."

"My point exactly. Not really something to write home about. Two years later, I'm sure many more have been added. Death surrounds you, Curtis." Kaylee shook her head and hugged Stephanie tight. "And it's not just the ones you cause. There is a woman who comes in my dreams. She is not alone and she tells me that you will protect me."

Kaylee paused as she prepared for the next part.

"Then I have a vision, shrouded in purple fog, where Stephanie and I are covered in blood. We are locked in a cave with others, underground." Kaylee stared directly in his eyes. "Henry Blackwell was not the only one that stalks you. He may have been the first, but he is not the last."

Curtis stared blankly at her. He reached up and stroked Stephanie's hair. "If we know what's coming, we can prepare. I don't fail, Kaylee."

She lowered her head and kissed the top of Stephanie's head. "Is it right for us to raise her surrounded by fear? Waiting for some lunatic to jump out and kidnap us?"

"What does Abigail say?"

"She said I needed to come clean. Lay all my cards on the table. I have struggled with this since before Steph was born."

"Do you know who they are? The ones that chase me?"

"I've seen some of their faces or identifying marks on them. One has a tattoo on his arm. It's a sword with a serpent wrapped around it. He is with Henry. They are connected in some way, but I am not sure exactly how. There are others. I saw a man comforting a blonde woman who cradled an infant in her arms. I didn't recognize them."

"Death has surrounded me my entire life. I have fought to triumph over evil again and again. I know it is asking a lot, but I'd do everything I can to keep you safe." He reached out and placed his hand on her arm that held Stephanie tight. "We took down Henry, and we can take down the rest. As long as we have each other, we will be safe."

"I love you, Curtis." Kaylee thought back to Abigail's words to separate the truth from fears. She knew what she must do. "I won't let fear dictate my decisions. I would be honored to be your wife." She leaned forward and kissed Curtis as Stephanie snuggled between her parents.

The perfect family, our perfect family. Kaylee read the thoughts in his mind and smiled. Was this the right choice? Time would tell.

Curtis opened the box and took out the ring and slid it on Kaylee's outstretched finger. "Now it's official."

"I like the design of the stones." She rocked her hand back and forth as she admired the ring. "A teardrop breaking through a plane, or more likely, as you picked it out, a blood drop."

"You read my mind."

~ CHAPTER 6 ~

KAYLEE'S FAIRY-TALE DAY

Kaylee looked out at the gardens from the bedroom window. She and Curtis had built a life together over the past three years. They had brought a daughter into the world, got engaged, and had planned the wedding of their dreams. Her vision had come to life: a small, sunset ceremony in the gardens of MacIntyre Farms. The guests, consisting mainly of friends as neither of them had many family members, were starting to gather.

From the upstairs window in the east wing, Kaylee looked out as their guests started to arrive and fill in the chairs. The sun began to set across the western sky. The shadows grew longer from the chairs lined up in the garden meticulously planted by his mother.

Dressed in her beaded silk gown, she reflected on the importance of this event. "Today is the day I marry my soulmate, the father of my child."

In the back of her mind, the question of what loomed ahead haunted her. She was content with her decision to continue this life with him. Her mother walked over and touched her daughter gently on the shoulder.

"Kaylee, it's time that we start heading downstairs."

Kaylee took one final look in the mirror. Her green eyes sparkled. Her exquisite gown highlighted her figure perfectly. Her dark hair curled meticulously around her face, over her shoulders and down her back. The cathedral-length veil pinned on the back of her head gave her a regal appearance.

"You are beautiful, and you're ready to marry the man of your dreams."

Kaylee smiled. She knew this was her destiny; this is where she should be at this time. This was the man that she would be with. She walked out of the room and headed to the garden. Confident in her decision and aligned with where she wanted to be, she stepped forward to meet her future head-on.

As Kaylee and her mom approached the French doors, she saw Curtis through the glass. He stood on the portico, waiting for the music to signal his departure. The band started playing and he walked down the aisle. Red and white roses tied with silver ribbon at the edge of each row of chairs greeted him as he walked past their family and friends. Twinkling lights draped meticulously in the trees and bushes created the magical setting in Kaylee's vision. The minister stood at the archway covered with lavender flowers. Curtis turned and faced the house, his right hand wrapped around his left wrist as he stood motionless waiting for his bride to appear.

Her maid of honor, Sarah, went next, guiding Stephanie in her role as flower girl. Guests were greeted by Stephanie grabbing handfuls of rose petals and jumping down the aisle as she littered them along the path and over the guests as well.

The bridesmaids made their way down the aisle and took their spot near the altar.

The minister raised his hand. "Please rise for the bride."

The music changed as Kaylee appeared at the French doors.

Curtis looked up the aisle towards his bride. Their eyes met.

Kaylee paused on the stone terrace focused on Curtis, her mother by her side. The two ladies, arm in arm, descended the limestone steps to the garden path that led to him.

Kaylee took a deep breath as her foot hit the crushed granite path. As the loose stone shifted under her weight, she struggled to keep her balance. Focused on the firm base underneath, she stood strong, confident, elegant as she walked step-by-step towards her groom as she glanced from left to right at their guests gathered together to bear witness to their union. She saw so many supportive, smiling faces as she approached the last few rows of guests, which reaffirmed her decision. As she glanced to the left, she caught Abigail's gaze.

Abigail simply smiled and nodded.

In Kaylee's mind, she heard her dearest friend and advisor's voice. *"You've made the right decision."*

Kaylee placed her fingertips on her chin, her hand flat and open as she let it fall forward as she gestured towards her friend the universal sign for thank you.

She looked ahead. Curtis stood in his black tuxedo, elegant blue eyes sparkling. Her friend and faithful assistant, Sarah, stood alongside Princess Stephanie. Their beautiful daughter stood in her sparkling, tooled dress with the basket of rose petals, her hair pinned back with white baby's breath with sprigs of lavender flowers tucked within. As Kaylee and her mom drew closer to the archway, Stephanie threw one more handful of rose petals that fell at Kaylee's feet, decorating the train of her gown.

The minister started the ceremony. "Dearly beloved, we are gathered here today in great celebration of the union of this man and this woman in holy matrimony."

The service was brief, elegant, and heartwarming. Kaylee had delegated most of the details to her maid of honor, Sarah, and her selections of flowers, music, and food were perfect. Stephanie added a jovial flair to the festivities. As she was just under two years old, her carefree ways and humorous demeanor radiated throughout the evening. Kaylee couldn't help but feel pride that Curtis was in Stephanie's life. He had been a positive influence, but the potential of that changing weighed heavy on her conscience. No time for that today. She pushed it out of her mind, squared her shoulders, and was ready to mingle with their guests. They were celebrating the present. The future would be here soon enough.

Not sharing Kaylee's need for parties and celebrations, Curtis was stressed at the reception. He was private, and she was in the public eye. He kept his emotions close, shielded from everyone, even her. He knew she read his thoughts, and he also knew how to manipulate them so she only saw what he wanted. Could psychopaths feel true emotion? He thought so. He felt pain, sadness, grief, happiness, love. He didn't know if he experienced emotions the same as others. He did know that he experienced things more vividly, more violently, than most.

As the night went on, they spent hours with their friends laughing and reminiscing. On the reception table sat pictures of Curtis's mom, Deborah; his grandparents, Darryl and Martha Mason; pictures of Kaylee and Curtis when they were children. The photographs of them in Winslow, Arizona, that sunny Saturday afternoon when their paths crossed for the first time. Pictures of happy memories. Noticeably absent, but rightfully so, were pictures of their fathers. Both Curtis's and Kaylee's fathers were not acknowledged nor represented formally.

The dessert table held a silver platter with Martha Mason's famous chocolate chip cookies.

"No event would be complete without Martha's cookies." Floyd, one of Darryl's oldest and dearest friends, grabbed several from the tray. "Darryl would be proud of the man you've become and the family you've created here. He's looking down on you. He's here with all of us in spirit."

Curtis got it. "I know he is. They all are."

Floyd reached inside his suit jacket pocket and pulled out a flask. He unscrewed the top. "Here's to them." He took a swig from the silver flask before he handed it to Curtis. "It's Deb's Mountain Oil."

A tear rolled down Curtis's cheek as he raise the flask to his lips.

"To Mom."

Curtis saw Kaylee watching from across the garden. He caught her eye and motioned for her to come over to the banquet table and take her rightful spot beside him.

As he held the flask in his hand, he turned to Kaylee.

"This was a recipe that Pappy made right after Mom died. He made it in her honor. He called it Deb's Mountain Oil." He offered the bottle for her to taste.

Kaylee looked at the flask. She admired the intricate etching on the case as she raised it in a tribute to the woman she'd never met.

"To Deb, thank you for bringing your son to me." She lifted the flask to her lips as the liquid entered her mouth.

Curtis watched with anticipation as a curious expression crossed her face.

"Did you taste the lavender?"

"It's got a sweet hint and definitely notice the lavender."

Floyd laughed. "Darryl thought that that would make the brandy sweeter. Be a nice touch and a nod to Deb's love of flowers and gardens."

"She certainly did exquisite work with the gardens here. Martha and I used to talk about that. I can't think of another place I'd rather get married than right here in her gardens," Kaylee added.

As the three of them continued to share stories and fun memories of people that were no longer with them in person, Curtis felt his mother's presence. Would he be the father and husband that Kaylee and Stephanie needed? Would he be able to shield them from the death that surrounded him? Maybe Kaylee was right with her concerns. Maybe he was never meant to have a family. His mother had taken her own life, and his father—Pappy took care of him. Would he be able to make Mom proud?

A purple butterfly fluttered joyfully, encircling all of them before landing on Curtis's hand. They all stared at the insect, gracefully moving its wings as the light twinkled off them. He looked up to the sky and raised his glass.

~ CHAPTER 7 ~
FIELD DAY

In the months that followed their wedding, Kaylee submerged herself in her writing. She spoke daily with her assistant, Sarah Johnson. Although no longer working for the *Chicago Tribune*, Kaylee had carved out a very successful freelance career for herself. Recently, she brought Sarah over to expand her team because she skillfully predicted her needs, often before Kaylee realized them herself.

Kaylee's successful piece on Henry Blackwell, The Serpent, earned her recognition as a top contender in investigative journalism. Sarah often reminisced about that day before Kaylee's trip to Phoenix, Arizona. They both hypothesized that it was a story that could catapult them into fame. Kaylee wrote pieces about politics and criminal investigations, intentionally taking a break from the missing people. Partly because of the personal loss they suffered, and partly because she feared what she may find. What may come to light about her husband.

At least once a month, Curtis would go out sometimes for just a few hours. Other times, he called up Barbara Hughes at Hughes Trucking and made a run out to the southwest desert. It was something they didn't speak about. They both knew what he was doing. Kaylee also knew she couldn't stop him.

It was the life that she'd signed up for. There were always consequences to your decisions. Sometimes the currency was too high to pay. Kaylee made sure that she kept her independence. She had a career; a way to provide for her and Stephanie if needed. She was good at hiding behind the mask, but she knew Curtis was better. He had learned from the best. She loved him not for the way he silenced her fears, but for the way his demons fed a part of her that she didn't even want to acknowledge.

* * *

Kaylee was already awake. Curtis stirred as he could tell her breathing was not relaxed. He opened his eyes and blinked as they adjusted to the light filtering through the window.

"Did you have another dream?"

"Nothing new." She rolled over to face him in the bed. "They're close. They're coming. I can feel it."

Curtis reached over and pulled Kaylee towards his chest. "I know." He ran his hand down her hair towards the small of her back. His fingers wrapped in the waves. "I can feel something too."

They lay there silently. Curtis's thoughts wandered. How was he to protect them? Could he make this go away? Could he ensure all of their safety? In his heart, he knew. It was hard, but the only logical option. They needed to go. The stalkers would follow him. He would lead them away from Kaylee and Stephanie. That was his last resort. They had talked about it and agreed. Kaylee and Stephanie would only leave if there was no other choice.

Curtis's thoughts drifted back to when he brought Kaylee into his secret world. She was an angel who searched for chaos, and he was a demon who sought peace. He thought that was the right decision, but he was beginning to doubt it. Maybe Pappy's way of never letting Grandma know his authentic self was a better option. Curtis couldn't go back, but he also knew he would not make that mistake again. His demons were a cross that he and he alone carried. But unfortunately, he had shown it to Kaylee, and now she, too, bore its weight. He knew he couldn't let Stephanie be impacted.

He kissed the top of Kaylee's head and continued to stroke her hair. Her breathing slowed as the morning sun filtered slowly into the bedroom. It was time to start the day. Just like the day couldn't hide from the sun, neither could they. He wasn't sure what the right answer was, but he knew they would figure it out together.

Kaylee's head rose as Curtis exhaled. "A little princess will be up soon," she reminded him.

"Our world is ruled by a two-and-a-half-year-old." Kaylee covered her eyes in a vain attempt to hide from reality.

"I can't say no to those striking green eyes." Curtis laughed. "She did inherit her mother's ability to manipulate with those eyes."

Kaylee tapped his chest with her hand as she scolded him. "We do not manipulate!" she said with a punctuated tone. "We merely strongly encourage."

They both laughed as the pitter-patter of little feet came running down the hallway towards their bedroom door.

A little knock and the door creaked open slowly. "Mommy? Daddy? Breakfast?" the little voice said as she pranced on tiptoes into the room.

Curtis's and Kaylee's eyes met. He didn't even need to say a word.

Kaylee smiled and whispered, "Touché."

"I'll be right there, princess. Meet you downstairs." Curtis swung his legs over the side of the bed.

"Okay, Daddy." Stephanie rushed towards the stairs.

"We better hurry." Kaylee stretched. "She'll be waiting at the table with good old Tucker right by her side."

As they made their way to the kitchen, sure enough, Steph sat poised with her fork at the kitchen table with faithful Tuck right beside her. His tail wagged as Kaylee walked over and opened the door to the patio.

"We are all creatures of habit," Curtis said as Tucker rushed out as soon as the door opened.

Kaylee left it open so he could return after his morning romp in the gardens, and it would save her a trip. Her life had become all about efficiency.

Kaylee answered him in thought. *"Remember, nothing's truly random. You just need to be in tune to the signs and patterns."*

Curtis shook his head as if he could remove her voice. "I hate when you do that."

The voice in his head simply responded, *"And that is why I do it."*

He wondered if Steph would inherit her mom's telepathic abilities. He knew she was special, he could sense that; they both could. But she was just too young to truly comprehend.

As he glanced out the open door, Curtis drifted back to growing up on the farm.

"I always loved getting up early to help feed the cows when I was a kid." He reached over and roughed Stephanie's hair. "I'm glad you will get to grow up with them as well."

Kaylee finished up the eggs and bacon, placed cut fruit in bowls, and carried it over to the table.

Stephanie had barely started eating her breakfast. "Can we go see the cows?" She raised the plastic cup to her mouth and took a sip of her milk.

"I think they were planning on doing some vaccinations this weekend. They should bring them up to the barn," Curtis said. "Be fun to hook up the wagon behind the tractor."

With over 300 acres, it was sometimes a challenge to find where the cows were grazing. When it was feeding time, they headed to the barn. Midday, they were scattered throughout.

"I think I remember hearing that there was a couple of new babies," Kaylee offered.

"Can we keep one of the babies?" Stephanie pleaded.

"We keep them till they grow up, and then we sell them at the market. There'll be new babies next year."

One day, she would figure out what the market really was and what happened to the cattle when they went there. His answer appeased her for now.

Curtis went out to the shed and hitched up the wagon to the tractor. He threw in a couple of hay bales and blankets for Kaylee and Stephanie to ride on in the back. Tucker scampered up the little ladder into the wagon and claimed his place at the front, right behind the driver's seat.

Kaylee helped Stephanie up the ladder and into the wagon filled with hay. Her eyes were wide with anticipation. "It's like a picnic, Daddy!"

"Daddy's always a gentleman." Kaylee took her spot on the blanket and patted the place beside her.

Stephanie followed her mom's request and sat on the hay beside her.

As they started across the fields in search for the cattle, the hair on Curtis's neck stood up. Someone was watching, he could feel it.

~ CHAPTER 8 ~

LET THE GAMES BEGIN

From the trees that edged the property, a pair of eyes peered out as the tractor pulled out of the barn. The wagon followed behind carrying his family across the field.

"Out for a hayride," a voice said. "Probably in search of the baby cow. They are in for a surprise." Laughter echoed through the trees.

He had been watching them for months; Curtis even longer. He was always fascinated by his history. Orphaned son of a wealthy rancher. Inherited the family fortune and business when he was barely eighteen years old. His family lineage traced back to the Masons, a family whose mystery ran deep in the Smokey Mountains of Tennessee.

Darryl Mason's sphere of influence stretched far and wide. With the tragic loss of their daughter, Debra MacIntyre, to her own hands and the mysterious disappearance of their son-in-law, Butch MacIntyre, over a decade ago, Darryl had taken a step back from public life, but the spotlight sought him out.

A few years back with the high-profile killing of a serial killer nicknamed The Serpent, they were front-page news once again. This time, the party had grown. Not only was his grandson, Curtis MacIntyre, front and center, a new member had joined their ranks. A reporter from the Windy City, Kaylee Smith-Roberts. It was obvious she was there to stay.

As he watched the tractor dip out of sight just over the hill, his voice growled low and deep. "You fear the darkness within your soul when you should be fearing me."

He walked back through the woods. There was no need to see their reaction. He would find out soon enough.

As Curtis drove the tractor across the field, Kaylee sat in the back making hand gestures of spiders climbing up waterspouts as they sang Stephanie's favorite nursery rhyme. She loved the innocence that Stephanie brought to their family. It made the darkness more bearable.

"I see some cows just up ahead."

"Mommy, do you think the baby cow is with them?" Stephanie exclaimed as she stood up to get a better look.

"Hopefully. Many times the mama cows will stay apart from the heard when the baby is really little," Curtis explained as the tractor carried them closer.

As the herd came into view, several heifers were grazing together, but they didn't see the new baby.

"There's a mama over there." Curtis pointed to the right. "Let's go check it out. Looks like she is looking at something lying in the grass. That may be the new baby taking a nap."

Curtis steered the tractor towards the cow. Kaylee and Stephanie leaned over the edge as they strained to see around the tractor. As they got closer, Kaylee realized that something was wrong with the baby.

The mother cow was standing over it pushing it with her muzzle.

"Oh Curtis!" Kaylee screamed as she grabbed Stephanie and shielded her eyes from the scene before them.

As he stopped the tractor and jumped down, Curtis ran over to the bloody calf and distraught mama cow.

"Whoa, mama." Curtis approached and laid his hand on the new mother's shoulder.

As he looked down at the baby, it was covered in blood. But more shocking was the fact that its head was severed from its body.

"This was no accident." He moved the head and examined the cut. "It's a clean cut."

"Curtis, we need to get out of here."

Stephanie had squirmed out of her mother's grip. Her mouth dropped open as she looked down at the baby cow and her dad with blood on his hands.

"What happened to the baby, Daddy?"

"It got hurt, angel," he said as he stood and patted the anxious cow again. "Something must have gotten it."

Curtis grabbed the radio from the tractor and called to the ranch hands to come to the far east pasture to pick up the calf.

Kaylee comforted Stephanie as she started to cry.

"It will be okay. The mommy cow was with her, and she's in heaven now," Kaylee reassured their daughter all the while fixing her gaze on the bloody handprints Curtis left on the cow, like an eerie brand on the cow's shoulder.

"Like with Grandma and Grandma Mason and Pappy too?"

"Yes. Now she's running through the fields in heaven." Kaylee wiped her tears from her cheeks. "I'm sure they were there to welcome her and give her lots of pets and hugs."

"Who did this?" Kaylee communicated to Curtis without words.

Curtis just shook his head.

As Kaylee tried to read his thoughts, she was blocked. Why did he only let her see what he wanted? Why was his trust not absolute? She is a part of his struggle; they will survive it together, if he'd only let her in.

Suddenly, she heard his calm voice in her head. *"If I let you read my mind completely, you would realize your ceiling is my floor. I thrive in a level of hell that you can't even imagine. If I let you in, you wouldn't stay. I am surrounded by fire, but you need to let me shield you and Stephanie from the flames."*

Kaylee smiled, hugged their baby, and whispered, "That is why I love you."

He knew more than he was telling. This she was certain. He would tell her when it was needed. Kaylee had grown accustomed to Curtis's secrecy. She didn't always agree, but she understood, which was enough.

Curtis was quiet and distant as he drove the tractor back to the barn. The slaughter that was set up for his family to discover had unnerved them both. Someone had gotten inside his circle, past the armor he had built around them.

◆————————●————————◆

As the day drew to a close, Curtis and Kaylee sat on the back patio, the sky set ablaze by the wondrous paintbrush of the setting sun. Stephanie played carelessly in the grass as she threw the ball for Tucker to tirelessly chase.

"That old hound will run himself into the ground for her." Kaylee sipped her wine.

"He is loyal for sure," Curtis responded. "He loves that little girl."

"I don't know what she would do without him."

He searched Kaylee's face for some sign of what she was thinking. Sometimes he wished he had Kaylee's telepathic powers. Sure, he could talk to her within their minds, but he had yet to perfect the mind-reading piece. He saw the edge of her lip curl ever so slightly. Damn, she must have heard his thought.

"When will you learn?" She laughed out loud.

Curtis shook his head. "You and your witchlike ways will always get the better of me."

They both laughed as Stephanie continued to play ball with the dog.

"Any ideas on the calf incident?" Kaylee asked.

"I have some thoughts. It is definitely a message. Someone has gotten close."

"Too close."

"Agreed." He studied his wife. "I will protect you both. Don't worry."

"It's not about worrying." She swallowed the last of her wine and sat the glass on the iron table. "It's about how much we can handle."

He tilted his head. "What are you saying?"

"I am standing on the line somewhere between giving up and seeing how much more I can take."

Curtis knew when to be silent so she doesn't hear his thoughts. Kaylee was teetering on the brink of leaving and this may just push her over the edge. He couldn't lose his family.

"We have been through so much." She turned and peered into his eyes, but her gaze cut straight to his soul. "You are drenched in the smell of blood and death like cheap perfume."

His eyes opened wide, not sure how to respond.

"Your hands are stained with the memory of countless victims you have murdered. Yet I trust them completely. They hold me at night. They wipe the tears from Stephanie's cheeks. I have loved you at your darkest moments. I stood beside you and watched you take a life. I have seen the scarves."

Curtis clasped his hands, resting his elbows on his knees, and lowered his head. Still remaining silent.

The guilt of how his burden impacted them was becoming too heavy to shoulder.

"You have set fire to the world around us yet vow to never let a flame harm us. That may be a life you want, but how is that living?"

Tears ran down her cheeks. He reached to wipe them away, but she grabbed his hand.

"No!" she said sternly. "You have brought this danger into our lives. You can't make it go away with a swipe of your hand. I knew when I met you it wouldn't be easy. How much pain do we have to go through before walking away is okay?"

"Fear will take over your world." His voice remained calm. "Fear is not real. It is a product of your thoughts."

"You bring *real* danger."

"Don't misunderstand, danger is very real. But fear is a choice. I choose not to deal in fear."

"I'm glad you separate the two. For Steph and me, I need to ensure her home is safe without the fear of some lunatic coming in. Today it was a calf, tomorrow it could be us."

"I understand," Curtis responded.

Kaylee knew he tried to keep his mind clear of thoughts. It was always a challenge when he was talking with Kaylee. She had several conversations going at different levels simultaneously.

She could hear his thoughts as they ran rampant in his head. Sometimes it was easier to let her in than say it out loud.

He mentally yelled, "*I just need one person to never give up on me. Just one to never leave. My mind says it's time to move on, but my heart screams hold on. It does not understand logic.*"

Kaylee reached for his hand. Her touch told him she heard him. Tears streamed down her face.

They were both struggling to come to terms with the truth. The path laid before them was not the one either wanted.

He waited for her voice to echo in his mind. Nothing came.

"It's better for you and Steph to go away for a while," he whispered quietly. "We can decide when the right time is."

His words hung long in the air as they rang loud in his ears.

"I promise to make sure you are safe, always. Even if that means I must stay at a distance."

She leaned back with a heavy sign of resignation.

"In the end, promises are just words," she said. "I don't want to leave, but sometimes you give us no choice. We need a plan. A way to disappear. You need to be careful and not bring on more spectators."

———•———

Over the next few months, they kept a low profile. Curtis took a few runs out to the West Coast for Hughes Trucking, but they mainly stayed close to the farm. The calves got bigger and as the days grew shorter, the time to start rounding them up for the market was drawing close. Kaylee liked this time of year. She often referred to it as the circle of life. Out with the old to make room for the new. But Stephanie was old enough now to notice when some were gone, and so they needed to be careful with their words.

"The cows are growing up big and strong," Curtis explained. "It is time for them to go on to their next adventure."

"They will have lots of fun! They like adventures!" Stephanie smiled, once again content with his explanation.

As the leaves became vivid with the colors of fall, the night air grew cooler and their evenings on the back porch overlooking the fields and barn ended early.

One night as they huddled on the couch together watching yet another princess movie, a dancing orange light reflecting in the windows caught Curtis's attention. Orange flames rippled up the sides of the barn.

"Oh shit, Kaylee!" he screamed as he jumped from the couch. "The barn!"

As Kaylee spun around, he was already at the door.

Stephanie cried, "Daddy! Are the cows in the barn?"

"I'll get them, sweetie," Curtis said as he flung open the door. "Don't worry, I'll save them!"

Kaylee yelled after him, "Be careful!" Then she sprinted to the phone and called 911.

After giving the operator their information, Kaylee held Stephanie and watched from the porch.

Curtis put his arm up to shield his face from the heat of the flames. He grabbed a hose and tried to fight back the flames so he could get to the doors and make sure the cows could get out. Soon, cows started running out of the barn across the pasture.

Thankfully, they were far enough away to not be able to hear the cows cry. The heat warmed Kaylee's face as she squinted against the bright light of the raging fire. In the distance, the sirens approached. Soon, the fire trucks arrived, and Curtis headed back towards them.

"Did you get them all out, Daddy?"

"I hope so. But it was already a really big fire." He lifted his shirt and wiped the soot from his face.

Kaylee wrapped one arm around his waist and kept the other around Stephanie.

They watched the flames engulf the barn as part of the roof started to cave in. The water from the hoses arched towards the barn as the firefighters tried in vain to save the old, wooden structure. They watched it collapse to a pile of smoking embers as the steam mixed with smoke rose from the fiery mass.

The fire marshal came over to explain what they'd found. It hadn't been an accident. After he left to go put up the crime tape and investigate the cause of the fire, Kaylee noticed Curtis was trembling.

Kaylee asked, "Are you okay?"

"Just a lot of memories about the last time there was an investigation at this farm." He attempted to smile, but she could tell it was forced. She loved that he tried to be strong for her.

"They will figure out what happened."

"Maybe it was a faulty electrical connection," Kaylee offered. Secretly, she knew it wasn't.

As the investigation concluded, the marshal showed up to take down the tape. "Mr. and Mrs. MacIntyre, the initial investigation is complete. It looks like this wasn't an accident. We found traces of accelerant in the barn."

"That's disturbing but not surprising." Curtis thanked the fire marshal. "Will you keep the case open?"

"The investigation is currently unsolved." He glanced between the two of them. "Do you know anyone that may want to do you harm?"

"That's a very long list," Kaylee said silently to Curtis.

"I can't think of anyone," Curtis said confidently. "Can you?" He looked at Kaylee.

She just shook her head. It was better she does not say anything out loud.

"Until we figure out any leads, I will make sure there are added patrols in this area." He jotted something down in his notepad. "Are you okay if they patrol around your house as well? You are pretty far back from the road."

"That would make Kaylee feel much more comfortable, I'm sure." Curtis reached for her hand. "Especially if I have to be out of town for business."

"Do you travel often, Mr. MacIntyre?"

"Not much anymore," Curtis responded as he brushed his fingers through his hair.

The marshal nodded as he continued to take notes in his notepad.

Kaylee took a step back towards the door. "We should get Stephanie to bed."

They bid each other good night and the marshal said he would be in touch as the investigation progressed.

"You can't control this anymore. It is bigger than both of us." Kaylee turned and walked back inside to put Stephanie to bed.

Curtis followed, watching her. He knew the time for her to leave was close and there was nothing he could say to change her mind.

~ CHAPTER 9 ~
TIME TO DISAPPEAR

The suitcase lay open on the bed. Curtis had taken a run out west and was gone for two weeks. The break gave her a chance to reflect on the recent events and figure out a plan. The messages had escalated. First, the baby cow in the field, then the barn burning; it was a matter of time before whoever it was got to them. They were no longer safe at the plantation. The tears ran down her cheek as she picked up the phone.

"Hello?" answered the voice on the other end of the phone.

"We need a way out." Kaylee's voice shivered.

"Are you in trouble?"

"They are getting too close for comfort. So Steph and I need a safe place to disappear for a while."

"Let me make some calls, and I'll let you know. Still can reach you the same way?"

"Sarah knows how to reach me and will pass any message along. It's best if we don't connect directly for a while."

"Understood," said the voice. "And Kaylee, I'll wire money to the account. I'm sure you will need cash."

"Thank you." She looked down at the list and checked off the box next to *Call Rupert*.

Rupert was an old friend she made while working on a missing persons case. He was heavily connected both inside and outside of law enforcement. She knew he would be able to get them new identities and a safe place to stay. She had reached out to him for informants in the past, but this was the first time she used his services personally. Neither Sarah or Kaylee had ever met him face-to-face, at least not knowingly. Maybe one day she would.

As Kaylee glanced down the list, there were still a couple of things that needed to be completed before they left. Curtis would be home in another four days, and they needed to be gone. The doorbell chimed, and she knew that was the delivery she had been waiting for.

As she opened the door, the driver greeted her. "Kaylee Smith-Roberts? I believe I have a car for you."

"Yes," she answered as he handed her the keys. "Thank you so much. It's all ready to go?"

"Full tank of gas, car seat in the back, and the paperwork including the title and insurance is right here." He handed her the sealed envelope.

She nodded as she took the documents and bid him farewell.

Kaylee walked down the steps and looked at the silver sedan that sat in the driveway. It was nondescript, plain; it was perfect. She had spent her whole life fighting to be recognized, and now all she wanted to do was disappear. It would be a hard transition, but one she must make. Her life and her daughter's life depended on it.

As she headed back inside, she remembered what Abigail told her once. It didn't matter what was in front of her because of the strength that was inside her. Stephanie would be up soon. She had completed everything she needed and her conscience was clear. She headed upstairs to get some rest.

He watched from the shadows behind the bushes as she came out and spoke to the man as he dropped off the car. He was familiar with the house from when his sister would speak of it so many years ago. He knew the property; he had been there so many times. It had been several months since he poured the kerosene in the barn and set it ablaze.

That was so easy, he chuckled as he remembered that night. Right under their noses. He had watched them from the edge of the woods as they sat on the patio as their daughter played in the yard. That should have been his niece in that yard. Rage boiled in his blood. She would have been a teenager now. He wondered if she would have had his sister's eyes. Curtis never gave her a chance. He took her life when he took his sister's.

As he wandered towards the back patio, he glanced in the windows. Everything was still. He knew Kaylee had gone upstairs. Now would be the perfect time.

He glanced down at the blood that dripped from the rabbit in his hand as he approached the back door. He slowly turned the knob and silently moved towards the basement door as he let the blood drip and create the path for her to follow. Like lambs to the slaughter. He knew she couldn't resist following the breadcrumbs, even if they were covered in blood.

After he placed the rabbit, he tapped his leg as Tucker approached.

"Come on, boy." He opened the door and let the dog out.

———————•———————

Several hours later, Kaylee awoke with Stephanie curled up beside her. She must have climbed into the bed while Kaylee slept. Kaylee quietly got up without disturbing the sleeping child and headed downstairs. There was much to do. She needed to leave before Curtis got back. That was the plan.

Something seemed off. As she got to the bottom of the stairs, she noticed the trail of blood drops on the floor.

"Tucker?" she called without a response. Her heart sank. Could someone have gotten inside? Was that Tucker's blood? Her legs started to shake and feel weak as they carried her across the room.

She kept calling out his name as she followed the trail. As she approached the basement door, chills shot up her spine. What if…. She couldn't even finish the thought.

As she reached for the basement doorknob, she paused a moment. What would she find on the other side? Was she ready to face it?

"Tucker?" she whispered as she hoped a whimper or some sound of life would return from the other side of the door.

The silence was deafening.

With each step down the staircase, she heard her heartbeat echo in her head as it pounded in her chest. As she reached the final steps, the humidity from the pool landed on her skin. She stopped and held her breath before she found the courage to unveil what lay around the corner.

The blood spots continued towards the pool. As she prepared herself for what was ahead, she took a deep breath, squared her shoulders, and forced her feet to take a step.

The red blood swirled in the pool. The animal carcass had sunk to the bottom. A slight scream escaped her lips before her hands covered her mouth. As her eyes took in the scene before her, she realized the body was too small to be Tucker. A feeling of relief flowed over her.

"Thank God!" she said out loud as her legs trembled.

She took several steps towards the edge of the pool and peered in. She squinted in an effort to bring the image at the bottom of the pool into focus.

What was it? The long ears. She didn't see a tail.

"Oh God! It's a bunny!" she gasped. "Who would do this? How did this happen?"

A distant bark caught her attention.

"Tucker?" she yelled as she turned to race back up the stairs.

Each step seemed like a mile. This was the longest staircase she had ever climbed. Her breathing was labored as she reached the top and turned towards the front door.

His bark came from the front yard. It sounded like it was moving away like he was chasing something or someone. She ran to the front door and flung it open, catching a glimpse of a car as it turned out of the drive. Tucker ran behind as he continued to bark.

"Tucker!" she called.

He stopped and looked back over his shoulder before he turned and headed back towards the house. It was definitely time for them to go.

As Tucker reached her side, she petted him. "Good boy. Should I take you with us?"

He just stared up at her as he wagged his tail.

That was all the confirmation she needed.

Kaylee knew she couldn't stay in the house that night. Their plan was for her to leave in two more days. But after this, she couldn't wait. Curtis didn't know where she was going. They thought it best that way. She picked up the phone to call him. As the phone rang, her hands grew sweaty, and her heart raced. She took deep breaths trying to calm herself.

When his voice answered, she broke down.

She heard him call her name as he asked what's wrong.

"He got inside," she said between gasps. "He put a bloody bunny in the pool. Oh God, I thought it was Tucker. I thought he got Tucker."

"Kaylee, calm down. You aren't making any sense."

"We can't stay here. It's not safe. We're leaving tonight," she managed to say between sobs.

"Is Tucker okay?"

"Tucker is okay. He chased the guy. I saw the car pull out on the road. I'm taking Tucker with us. He will warn us."

"Okay, Kaylee," Curtis said. "I'll come now."

"No, Curtis. You can't be near us. I shouldn't have called. You can't look for us. Not now. Not yet. I'll let you know when it's safe. You will hear from me but promise you won't come after us."

"I will try."

Kaylee knew she needed to end the call. She needed to get everything packed and loaded. They needed to leave as soon as it was dark.

"Goodbye, my love," she said as he cried on the other end of the phone.

~ CHAPTER 10 ~

A Mother's Intuition

Curtis struggled as he learned to live alone again. He had friends, but it wasn't the same. He tried to stay busy and picked up a monthly trucking route to Arizona. As he walked through the house, the emptiness was deafening. His footsteps echoed as the sound rattled around the uninhabited rooms. He welcomed the familiarity of the surroundings, but it lacked life. He longed for the pitter-patter of Stephanie's feet. The unrelenting requests from Tucker to go in and out. The simple fact that Kaylee was there by his side.

He had built walls to keep others out. To protect his heart. He didn't tear them down, but she climbed over to see what was inside. Once she was inside, he changed. He stopped trying to belong to a world that never fit him. Together, they created their own world, a family, a life.

Somewhere along the way things changed. Life was no longer about living; it was about surviving. He remembered when he saw his reflection in the eyes of the Serpent. "How could you kill a monster without becoming one yourself?" Her words resonated in his soul. He had become a monster. He wasn't exactly sure when the transformation happened. Maybe he always was. Did it happen the summer in 1983 when he killed Candice Jordon and her unborn child? Did it happen when he killed the three ladies in California? Was it any of the almost two hundred people that lost their lives at his hands? Was it when he killed the Serpent that day in the woods in Arizona? Did it even matter? He was fed by transforming pain into power.

Curtis would not apologize for who he was. The need to kill was a part of him. Kaylee had seen behind the wall and has accepted it. Mind, body, and soul. Everyone was someone's monster, there was no changing that. But it was up to you what type of monster you became.

It was the others. Those were the ones that haunted them. That stalked them. The visions Kaylee saw in her dreams. They were the bad ones, the villains. The monsters that must be stopped. It wasn't his demons they needed to conquer.

As Curtis's circle got smaller, his purpose clarified. He fought not because of hate for those on the path in front of him but for the love of those who stood behind him.

Kaylee learned how to be strong without him physically by her side. No one knew how much she cried that day. It may not have killed her to leave, but a piece of her died that day. As she watched Stephanie play with her doll on the living room rug with Tucker by her side, she realized they would be okay. Not because of what she had been through, but because of what was inside of her. Like the moon, she had a dark side that even the stars couldn't cast light upon. She had a side so cold the sun couldn't warm it.

There was no light without darkness, no hate without love, no pain without joy. Whatever was reflected outward always cast a shadow behind for others to see, if they looked. She presented a quiet confidence to the outside world. Yet he saw the weak, scared child that reflected in her shadow. That was why she wanted to be loved by him.

He saw demons lurking in the shadows of her secrets. He saw past her mask when others couldn't. He offered something she was afraid to ask for. He invited her to stand by his side, as his equal. His demons circled them both as they danced.

She felt comforted in the fact that he was not afraid of his own truth. Kaylee yearned for that. Curtis protected his family, not because they were weak, but because they were important.

But this was where they needed to be right now. Distance from Curtis made her feel safe in some ways but not in others. She knew Curtis would come for them, but she didn't expect it so soon. As she made dinner that night, she could feel he was close. She stared out the window above the kitchen sink.

"Where are you?" she whispered, secretly hoping he would respond.

If he was out there, he would hear her as she sent him her thoughts.

"The visions are clearer. There's a link to your past. They seek vengeance. They look to right a wrong."

She waited for a response in her head. As the silence continued, her eyes frantically scoured the tree line. Should she let Tucker out? If he was out there, he would find him. She persuaded herself to stay inside. Now was not the time. It was too soon.

"I saw a baby." She hoped he could make sense of the clues that were meaningless to her. "One is close to you. Perhaps too close. Be careful."

Tucker rubbed against her leg and whimpered softly as he peered out the door towards the woods.

"This is a walk we must make alone." She wiped her hands on the kitchen towel. "Those are the journeys that make us stronger. I know he is out there in the wild. Some people are not meant to be tamed. He will run until he finds someone just as wild to run with. Until then, he is a lone wolf."

Kaylee patted Tucker on his head. "Come on, boy. What's Princess Stephanie up to?" They walked towards the living room.

Stephanie sat quietly on the rug as she played with her dolls. Kaylee curled up on the floor beside her.

She was content for now. She needed to get some rest as tomorrow was another day and the demons were close. A battle was coming. Perhaps her dreams would bring the clarity she sought.

◆———◆———◆

The scenes swirled recklessly in her head. Starting and stopping abruptly, violently, as she tossed and turned in her sleep. She watched from the outside like a voyeur at a peep show. They were out of order. Some from the past, some yet to be. Her eyes darted side to side as pictures flew at her. Woods, fire, people. Screams of terror from his victims rung in her ears. Were they all his? So many voices. So many deaths.

She focused on the fog as it started to clear. Something was there, moving towards her. She struggled to make it out. To bring it into focus. She wished a strong wind would come and clear out the fog, but alas, the air was still in her dream.

Then she saw them, ghost-like aberrations. They were as plentiful as stars in the Arizona sky. More than she could count. They floated through the fog across the field of grass. She didn't know where they were going, but she knew they held the answer she sought. Were they Curtis's victims? Could he have killed so many women? She searched for some resemblance to the photos she still had in boxes. Missing women, each with their own story. Some had been told, more she wanted to tell, and countless others that yearned to have a voice.

She realized they were headed towards a clearing surrounded by a peaceful light. She tried to run to see what was there. To get there first. The harder she ran, the farther away they were. She felt her breath become labored as the vivid images flashed in her eyes. Suddenly, a flash appeared, then everything went black.

She heard a sound. Soft and sweet, like the coo of a dove. She floated above a circle of women surrounding a basket. Kaylee strained her eyes to make out what was in there. It was piled with cloth. She saw it moving as she slowly got closer. As things came into focus, she noticed light reflected off one of the women. Her hair was long and blonde. She was thin and tall, dressed in a white, flowing gown and she had a scarf.

Kaylee focused on the scarf. Had she seen it before? The pattern seemed familiar. As she stepped forward towards the basket, her hands came into view. The billowy sleeves of her gown fell away and Kaylee noticed some red markings on her wrists. Even in her dreamlike trance, she squinted to make out what they were. Ligature marks maybe? She had been tied up. As the woman's hands reached the basket, she picked up something wrapped in the cloth.

A pain shot through Kaylee's stomach as the woman in the vision collected her treasure. She instinctively knew. In her sleep Kaylee reached for her stomach and cradled it, protective. This woman had been pregnant and that was her child.

As she watched the scene unfold before her eyes, the woman started to turn towards her. She held her breath as the face came into view. It did not belong to the woman. It was familiar. She had seen him many times. He had been at the house, at their wedding. He was there shortly after Stephanie was born. Curtis had known him for years. They had met in trucking school. He was from Virginia.

She gasped and found herself sitting up in her bed, drenched in sweat. Disoriented, Kaylee wiped her face with the bedsheet as she struggled to catch her breath. The pieces were starting to make sense. She went through the missing women pictures in her mind. She knew the scarf was something she'd seen before. As her mind raced at lightning speed, she started to talk out loud.

"That scarf belongs to one of the women. But which one? Think, Kaylee, think."

She got up and went to her closet. She moved her pair of red-soled Louboutin black pumps to the side as she retrieved the shoebox nestled behind. She climbed back in bed and lifted the cover off the box. Dozens of pictures were housed inside.

She spread them out on the bed, combing through them, searching for the scarf. She was down to the final few pictures.

"It has got to be in here somewhere." She closed her eyes and visualized the woman in her dream.

Her eyes opened, and she scanned the pile of photographs. One was upside down. She read the name on the back.

"Candice Jordon."

"Could it be? That was the first lady Curtis killed when he was barely eighteen." Kaylee put her hand on the photograph, afraid to turn it over and discover what she already knew was true.

"Was she pregnant?" Kaylee couldn't remember if she was or not. It seemed like a small detail, but obviously to the spirits it wasn't.

Her hand trembled as she slowly lifted the picture. She turned it away from her so the other side remained a mystery. She hesitated, then in a quick motion she flipped it right side up on the bed.

"Bingo!" The picture did not disappoint. Not only was the scarf the one she saw in her dream, but the lady was the same. Her blonde hair, her build. She never saw her face, but she knew it was her.

"But what is the connection to Curtis's friend?" Kaylee could not figure this out. "That mystery is for another day."

She not only knew who was after them, she knew why.

~ CHAPTER 11 ~
FRIEND OR FOE

Curtis stretched and reached over to shut off his alarm. He turned on the cold water and mixed in just a bit of hot. A cool shower was just what he needed to break through the exhaustion he felt from his trip to check on Kaylee and Stephanie. He had watched them from afar. His wife, daughter, and even his dog were miles away, yet never far from his thoughts. Even though he hated Kaylee's ability to speak to his mind and read his thoughts, it did have its benefits.

He had watched them for days before she realized. He perfected this skill over the years when he stalked his victims. He needed to understand who they were, their patterns. Making things appear random took a lot of calculated planning. That was something he was very good at. Kaylee was too. It was nearly impossible for him to stay several steps ahead of her.

From the edge of the woods that night, he decided to let her in. He opened his mind and thoughts and knew she would not disappoint. As he saw her in the kitchen window, he heard that sweet voice enter his head asking where he was. He listened to her words. The message he pursued lay between the lines. The space in between what she said. As she told him about her visions, the faces she saw, he knew instantly the link. He prayed she would figure it out. His father always said, "Keep your friends close but your enemies closer." This was one thing that Dad actually got right.

He planned to catch up with his friend Anthony, the Chantilly Kid from Virginia, later in the day. First, he'd take care of some other pressing business. He needed to feed his inner demon with an appetizer, then he could deal with the devil before him.

He drove to Hughes Trucking and climbed into his rig. This was a short trip just across the Tennessee line and back. He planned to meet up with Anthony on the way back.

As the gentle, undulating hills of central North Carolina gave way to the Smoky Mountains, he rolled down the window. The sweet scent of the last of the wildflowers always put a smile on his face. Memories of his mother drifted into his thoughts. Her love of flowers persisted until her dying breath. The anger started to bubble up from the pit of his stomach. Calm, deep breaths, she would say. He exaggerated the sound as he inhaled and exhaled slowly as his heart continued to beat hard.

He became frustrated with himself for not realizing the connection before. He prided himself on connecting the dots and seeing the small details. This was a big miss. Looking back, it was clear. Nothing was truly random, Kaylee always told him. You just weren't looking for the right clues.

As he pulled into the familiar truck stop along Route 40, he remembered the one that got away. Kristi with a *K* and two *I*'s. He laughed. She didn't really escape. He let her go. Which was entirely different. No one had ever escaped him. They definitely had unfinished business.

Kristi was young, much younger than him, but she was an old soul. She fit his profile, but something stopped him that night. He never experienced that before nor since. She was truly different. It was strange seeing her the day that Stephanie was born, but he was glad he did. He had kept in touch with her off and on over the years since their paths crossed that day in the hospital. It wasn't very regular, but they met up for drinks, for lunch, for walks in the park. They shared memories from their past.

Kristi had grown up on the periphery of society. She carved her story out of dark alleys, railroad boxcars, and sleazy strip clubs. He grew up with a silver spoon, china from France, and a house with a staff of six. He played with the gardener's son, learned Spanish from the cleaning staff, and took swimming lessons from the pool boy his mother hired. Then the spring of his senior year, his whole world crumbled. His mother killed herself, he killed his dad's mistress and her unborn child, his grandfather killed his father, and he took to the road.

He traveled that lonely road for a decade until things started to change. At first it was so subtle,

Curtis barely realized what was occurring. As he reflected, the trigger seemed to begin when he met Kristi in that truck stop in Tennessee. Over the course of the next six months, he met Kaylee, lost his grandmother, killed his stalker, and Pappy died.

Sometimes things have a way of showing back up. His and Kristi's paths had crossed again in that hospital for a reason. He knew he couldn't let her go again. He also knew there was something she was hiding from him. If only he could figure it out.

As he sat in his truck, it didn't take long for a woman to stroll across the parking lot. He watched her as she walked with purpose towards the row of parked trucks. Not the one he was looking for. She was too confident. He needed someone meeker.

The Universe never failed to deliver. A dark-haired lady entered his field of vision. She had a scarf tied around her waist as a belt. The long ends swung back and forth as she walked. With her head lowered, shielding her eyes from the passersby, she had secrets to hide. He read her body language. This was one he could help.

He timed his entrance perfectly. As she neared his truck, he walked around the front with his logbook in his hand. His eyes diverted so when he ran into her it appeared unintentional.

"Excuse me." The words flowed easily from his lips as his strong hands reached out to steady her and he dropped the logbook on the ground.

"Sorry, I wasn't watching where I was going." The fragile creature answered as she quickly looked away.

"My fault completely. Are you okay?"

She nodded and shyly turned towards him like a scared deer.

"Are you sure? You seem a little shaken."

"Maybe a little, but it's not you." She looked cautiously around.

"Someone you're looking for?"

"Someone I hope not to find."

Curtis curled his lip slightly. His selection process never failed him.

"Let me walk with you." He moved to her side, slightly behind her shoulder. "You seem a little concerned."

Her shoulders dropped as she raised her eyes. "I would appreciate that." She pointed towards the adjacent parking lot. "My car is just over there."

They walked towards the edge of the truck stop making small talk along the way. Once they reached her car, Curtis made sure she got in and it started before he sent her on her way.

"Thanks!" she said from the open car window as she smiled and backed out of the parking spot.

Curtis took note of her license plate number and her car, a silver Honda Civic. He turned and headed back to his truck. She had a head start, but he was a professional.

He pulled out onto the highway and keyed his CB mic. "Breaker, breaker one nine, looking for a little rabbit in a silver Honda Civic. Come on back."

His fellow drivers quickly came back. "One just passed me. Long, dark hair. New York plates."

"That's the one. What mile marker?"

Curtis was only a few miles behind her. His foot instinctively pressed down on the accelerator as the diesel engine groaned under the weight of the trailer. Soon, he spotted the silver Honda up ahead. She would need to stop soon for fuel. He noticed the needle was barely over a quarter of a tank when she started up her car.

She was scared and running from someone, so she obviously was distracted. Thus why she didn't get gas when she stopped before. He knew the exits very well along this route, and they were not heavily traveled for the next hundred miles. His patience was rewarded as her turn signal started to flash. The adrenaline surged in his blood as he guided his truck off the exit.

He parked the truck at the fast-food restaurant and kept his distance. He watched her head into the store and come out with a bag. As she started to pump the gas, her head twisted back and forth as if searching for signs of danger. When she got back into her car and pulled away, Curtis was surprised she turned left and didn't head back towards the interstate. Could he be so lucky?

She drove a few miles down the road and pulled off by a little outcropping of trees. Curtis smiled. He drove past her car and parked around the bend in the road. She wouldn't see his truck from there. He slowly walked down towards her car, the trees offering the perfect camouflage.

As he came up along the back passenger side of her car, he saw that she had her eyes closed and was lying in the seat. He tried the back door of the Civic. It opened easily. He slid silently into the back seat. She didn't move.

He watched her chest rise up and down, rhythmically. The scarf was tied neatly around her waist, threaded through the belt loops. It would be hard to get off quickly. He would have to just use his hands for this one.

As he studied her, she stirred. He held his breath.

Like a lion, he pounced swiftly, mercilessly. His hands wrapped around her delicate neck. Startled, she tried to sit up, but it was too late. She was his prey. Her eyes widened as she peered up at him and realized what was happening.

"I will make sure he doesn't ever find you."

She dug her nails into his hands and arms trying in vain to get free. She kicked with her legs but nothing helped. She was powerless against his strength.

"You bitch!" He looked down at the blood on his arm where her nails clawed him. "Look what you've done!"

He viciously yanked her into the back seat, blood dripping from his arm onto the cushion. She fought tirelessly for her life.

"Accept it, bitch. You will not survive." He dug his fingers into her flesh.

Her gasps punctuated the sound of her trachea being crushed. Her movements jerked, the fluidity gone as the lack of oxygen took its toll.

Curtis wrapped his leg over her as he held her down.

Finally, she was again still. Her eyes were dark and cold. Her lips a bluish tint. He raised his arm to his mouth and sucked off the blood.

This one was messy. He would need to do something with her car. He was too far from home to take it there. He climbed into the driver's seat and headed towards his truck. He grabbed a screwdriver from his small toolbox. He drove the car back into a nearby forest and ran it into a tree. He untied the scarf from her pants and pulled it free before he placed her in the driver's seat. He punctured the gas tank and as the fuel poured out, he lit a match and threw it towards the car. As he walked back to the truck, he felt the heat from the fire.

He rolled down the window, and the smell from the fire entered his nostrils. He heard the explosion as he pulled on to the interstate. The wind blew the lingering smell of gasoline mixed with death from his clothes and his conscience as the sirens from the approaching fire engines rang in his ears. He knew they would never link him to her. There would be no evidence to investigate. It would be ruled an unfortunate accident.

Now it was time to get to Tennessee. This errand had taken more time than he had allotted, and he was running late.

He rolled across the Tennessee line a little ahead of schedule. He made good time. The engine went silent, but the voices in his head screamed. What was Kaylee and Steph doing? They were his driving force, his lifeblood. Everything he did was for them. Tonight, he would confront his rival. He was clad in armor from the past and thought it would protect him. Anthony had never experienced the depths of hell where Curtis thrived.

Curtis sat patiently as he waited for his arrival. He played this conversation over in his mind many times the past weeks. Each time it took a different path but ended the same. Curtis suddenly heard her voice in his head.

"He's here!" Kaylee screamed.

~ CHAPTER 12 ~
THE MISSING LINK

The room was dark. The sound of her breathing filled the air. Kaylee sat motionless, attuned to every signal. The metal felt cold in her hand. Kaylee wasn't a fan of guns, but Rupert thought it best that she was protected when he prepared the cabin. Her eyelids were heavy from lack of sleep, but she pushed the fatigue aside. She sensed the end was close, and she needed to be there to greet it head-on when it arrived.

The silent creak of the door was deafening as it shifted the pressure in the room. She closed her eyes and listened to the soft footsteps as they approached Stephanie's bedroom door. Tucker lifted his head. Kaylee lowered her hand, palm facing him, her fingers outstretched. He remained still and quiet.

Her eyes focused on the doorknob to the exclusion of everything else. She only had one shot. It needed to be perfect. She played the various scenarios over in her head. Each path different but resulted in the same ending.

She sent a message to Curtis. She knew he would come, but it would be over before he arrived. It was up to her. Their future, their lives, rested solely on her shoulders. The gun in her hand was the only thing that stood between her daughter growing up with a mother and following her father's path.

The seconds ticked by in slow motion. As the footsteps stopped, she knew he was directly outside the door. Was his hand on the knob? Would he take the bait?

The moonlight dimmed as clouds obscured its glow. Even in the diminished light her eyes remained laser focused on the knob. She noticed the intricate carving on its surface. The way the finish was worn off. The type of wear that could only be achieved after years of use. How many hands had turned that knob to enter the room? How many people had slept peacefully here? Would that safety be forever marred by the event that was about to take place?

She heard the lock jingle. Every muscle in her body tensed. Her finger moved to the trigger as she slowly rose from the chair. Her legs felt wobbly, but they held her weight. She lifted the gun, peered down the sight on the barrel, and lined it up with her impending target.

The knob started to turn. She held her breath and waited. It turned completely clockwise until the egg-shaped knob was parallel to the floor. The door moved inwards, slowly.

She saw the tip of his shoe as he cautiously entered the room. The sweat on her palms made it hard to hold the gun. She stood frozen like a stone statue. Time stood still.

At that exact moment, she understood what Curtis felt that day in the desert. Her inner warrior had arrived and she was fierce. A force to be reckoned with. The thought of Stephanie becoming collateral damage the way Pappy had, terrified her. That was a risk she was not willing to take.

His foot pushed past the edge of the door as it swung gently open. The silhouette appeared before her. The darkness of the room gave her cover.

She saw the moonlight reflect off the knife as he held it low and near his waist. Pointed out, ready to strike. His head turned as he glanced around the room before his eyes locked on Stephanie's bed. Her instincts were spot on. He headed straight for her daughter.

As he took a step towards the bed, Tucker pulled his ears back, lowered his head, and stretched out his neck. He was preparing for battle as well. His lips parted slightly as his teeth glistened, showing the wolf within.

Kaylee curled her index finger around the cold metal trigger and as he reached for the blankets on the bed, she squeezed.

A flash erupted from the muzzle of her gun as the bullet cut through the air with laser accuracy. Tucker stood growling, baring his teeth. In slow motion, she could almost see the bullet's trail as it left the metal tube and began the ten-foot journey to reach its destination.

He turned towards her and lunged, meeting the bullet along his path. It tore a hole through his chest. The force in which it struck threw him back on the bed. He landed hard on the blankets covering the contents underneath.

The clouds parted as moonlight filled the room. His shirt was soaked with crimson liquid that poured from his body. The cold, hollow stare in his eyes told her the bullet had done its job. As she approached the bed, she kept the gun pointed directly at his head, her fingers wrapped around the trigger.

Should she add a second bullet for insurance?

No need.

She sent a second message to Curtis. *"It's over."*

His love filled her heart as his voice rang through her head. *"It was Anthony. I'm so sorry."*

"We are safe. He can't hurt us anymore."

"I'm coming," he said.

<hr>

After the police left the cabin, Kaylee picked up the phone and called Rupert.

"You definitely have some strong premonitions," Rupert said as she heard Stephanie in the background. "I heard the dispatch call go out over the scanner. Sounded like you were a pretty good shot as they just asked for the coroner."

"I had the element of surprise on my side," she said with a touch of ego. "I hear Stephanie. Can I talk with her?"

Kaylee was happy to hear Stephanie's voice. It was a last-minute decision to send Stephanie somewhere else. She knew to trust her instincts even if she didn't completely understand the reason.

She had placed some of Stephanie's stuffed animals and a doll in her bed covered with blankets. When Anthony had started towards the bed, she knew she made the right decision. Rupert was more than willing to take Steph for as long as she needed. Kaylee was a little apprehensive as she had never met Rupert in person.

When she arrived at the hotel lobby where they met for the exchange, her fears were unwarranted as Stephanie took to him right away. He was like a big teddy bear. His grizzly beard and rounded belly made him resemble one too.

"When are you coming to get me, Mommy?"

"In a few days, baby. I have some stuff to clean up here. I will have a surprise for you when you get home."

"A surprise?" The squeal of excitement that escaped Stephanie's mouth made Kaylee pull the phone from her ear. "What is it?" she impatiently asked.

"I can't tell you or it wouldn't be a surprise." She laughed as she continued to talk to her daughter and hear about all the fun stuff she and Rupert had planned.

As Kaylee ended the call, she told Rupert that she was certain that Curtis would show up and that she would be in touch about coming to get Stephanie in a few days, as her room was a bit of a mess at the moment.

Kaylee started to clean up the room, remove the bed, and get things put back together. The police had arranged for a cleaning service to decontaminate the scene, but she knew the room needed to be redone completely before Stephanie could move back in. She had already ordered a new bed and mattress and would go shopping later to pick out new bedding. Something fit for a princess.

As she settled down on the couch as the day drew to a close, she heard the familiar sound of a car pull into the driveway. He was here.

She didn't reach the door before it opened and Curtis rushed in.

"Babe, I'm so glad you are alright." He swept her up in his arms and squeezed her so tight she struggled to breathe. "Where's Stephanie?"

"I sent her with a friend. I had a feeling." Her words trailed off.

Curtis shook his head.

"I was supposed to meet Anthony last night for dinner. As soon as I got your message that someone was here, I knew."

He let Kaylee go as he paced back and forth across the room.

"I should have figured it out. I don't know how I missed it."

"How could you have known?"

"I figured it out. That it was him who was doing all these things. I fell right into his trap. I was so focused on being the hero, I didn't realize I was the one being set up."

"Don't blame yourself." She reached out and touched his arm.

"It is my fault!" he shouted as he pulled his arm away. "I am supposed to protect you. I failed. Once again, I failed."

Kaylee stood and watched him.

"I gave him the perfect alibi. Dinner with the serial killer husband while he goes after the wife and child. How could I be so stupid?" He ran his fingers through his hair. "Do you know who he is?"

Kaylee was confused by his question. "Your friend from trucking school, Anthony Jordon."

As soon as she said the name out loud, she realized the connection. Jordon. Candice Jordon. The baby was her unborn child.

Her mouth dropped open. "Is he related to Candice?"

Curtis nodded. "Her younger brother. I didn't put it together until recently. He was out for vengeance. I told him about the cow and the barn fire. I told him about meeting you in Winslow. He was at our wedding, for Christ's sake."

"It will be okay." She wrapped her arms around his waist. "As long as we have each other."

He pulled her hand towards his mouth and kissed it gently. "We better get Stephanie's room cleaned up. I think you made quite the mess in there."

"And we clean up our messes together, remember?"

"Always."

~ CHAPTER 13 ~

BLISSFULLY UNAWARE

The next few weeks were pure heaven. Like old times. Curtis enjoyed the time spent with Stephanie and Kaylee. He even enjoyed old Tucker. If only he could stop the world right here and just relive it over and over. This is paradise, his nirvana. He missed the old times. He longed for them. They had created the perfect family on the farm. He had let it slip away. More accurately, chased it away.

As he looked back on the last decade he knew Anthony, the pieces fell into place. They were about the same age. Anthony was a little older. They immediately connected over the recent deaths of women in their lives. They joked about how they passed away so close in time maybe there was some connection. Curtis always knew that even in humor, a vein of truth existed. Sometimes you couldn't see the forest for the trees.

Over the past few years they had spent even more time together. Anthony had been to the farm. He had slept in their home. He had come to their wedding. He'd held their daughter. Curtis saw that picture in his mind.

Stephanie had just been born. They had been home a month, and The Kid had swung by in his rig. They both had welcomed him in. Tucker growled at him when he saw him through the window as he approached. It seemed strange at the time, but Curtis brushed it off as Tucker being protective of the new baby. He should have listened more closely.

He sat at their kitchen table. Kaylee placed Stephanie in his arms and he smiled at her. Curtis remembered the words he said to her: "The circle of life. It's fate in the end. The divine purpose. One giveth and the other taketh away." He looked up from the baby, looked straight at Curtis, and said, "There's always another one down the road."

It seemed strange at the time. Even Kaylee said something about it after he left. Curtis trusted his friend. The bad stuff was harder to believe, even for a serial killer.

Curtis blamed himself for what happened. The law of attraction; you attract what you manifest. In the end, he was a prolific killer. He had accepted that and so had Kaylee. Somehow, she rationalized that he was worthy of her love and her heart. He wasn't so sure. Eventually, when you wore two masks long enough, you forgot which was real. Were they really masks? The line between reality and fiction started to blur. His mind slipped into a new space so slowly, he didn't even notice. Darker than anything he had ever experienced before. An abyss so vile that even he was an outcast.

He found comfort in this new world. He played with Stephanie during the day. The perfect father, the doting husband. After Kaylee fell asleep, he would sneak out to hunt.

He had discarded his rules. There was no need for them. It was no longer about justifying why he killed. He didn't care to save them from imminent pain. He sought to squelch his own pain. His kills became more violent.

Under the cover of night, he slipped out of the cabin. The cool mountain air smacked him in the face. Kaylee had picked the perfect location to get away. The isolation served him well. His mission was clear. He was the mighty hunter and would only return home with his kill.

He set off on foot. He carried a knife. The knife that the Chantilly Kid had brought into his daughter's room. He believed he intended to kill her with it. Thankfully, Kaylee had other plans that night. The knife's purpose was to kill, and Curtis would not disappoint. He would allow it to fulfill its mission, again and again and again.

He walked through the woods to the parkway. The low wooden guardrails marked his arrival. People hiked these trails year-round, often camping for the night in random places. He started on his journey. His eyes searched the darkness until he saw a glow of the last embers of the campfire off in the distance.

Slowly, he approached the campsite. A single backpack propped up against a rocky outcropping. A small tent set up amongst the trees. It was peaceful. He watched the person sleep. The sound of his breathing oscillated through the darkness.

Hundreds of stars glistened as they burned millions of light-years away. Some of the light came from stars that had already been extinguished. The light traveled such a long distance, the fact that its light source had faded would never be realized in our lifetime. Or even in those of our children.

As he peered in the tent, another light will be snuffed out tonight. This one much closer to home.

He crouched low near the edge of the tent. The scruffy beard around the man's face confirmed he was a hiker and had been on the trail for weeks. No one expected to hear from him. He would not be missed anytime soon.

The light of the moon coupled with the glow cast from the dying embers gave him a sinister appearance. Curtis clenched his jaw and raised the knife above his head.

With a mighty scream, he plunged the knife deep into the man's chest. Blood spurted out as he raised it above his head before plunging it into his chest again and again. The man struggled as he awoke. A monster was attacking him. He tried to fight and get away, but his attempts were futile. Curtis saw the shiny metal of the blade in the man's hand. He had a knife of his own. This enraged Curtis, and his violence escalated. Blood drops flew from the knife as its path through the air quickened. He was unable to stop. The knife plunged deep as it ripped through this skin and scraped against bone.

Curtis surveyed the scene. He was covered in blood. His arms were scraped like he had been mauled by a wild cat. The tent was speckled with blood splatter. The man lay motionless still in his sleeping bag, saturated with blood. His eyes were open, his mouth as well. Curtis didn't know how many times he had swung the knife. It didn't matter. He had defeated his prey.

He stood. The moon was almost full. He tipped his head back and howled. A call from another lone wolf echoed back in the darkness. Curtis smiled as he headed back to the cabin following the low, wooden guardrails along the road. He didn't try to hide the bodies anymore.

The next morning, they gathered around the breakfast table as the television played in the background.

"In local news, another body was found along the Blue Ridge Parkway," the voice from the speaker said.

"They seem to be more frequent lately." Kaylee picked at her eggs.

"Maybe there is a killer on the loose."

"Maybe?" Her head shook at his comment. "What's the chance of two killers hanging out in the mountains?"

"There are two right here." He knew she suspected it was him.

"Curtis!" She flicked a piece of bacon at him.

"Just kidding, my love." He expertly swatted it down towards his plate before picking it up to eat.

Stephanie laughed at the silly antics of her parents.

"Good thing she is blissfully unaware," Kaylee whispered to Curtis in his head.

◆━━━━━●━━━━━◆

The mood in the small mountain town was tense. Five hikers were murdered in the last month. The police force was strapped for resources as they tried relentlessly to protect the community. Kaylee wondered if Curtis had anything to do with this. It wasn't his style at all. He had been different lately. He had changed so drastically it was hard to pinpoint exactly what had changed.

He appeared very relaxed and overly confident as they went into town to take care of their weekly errands. As the townspeople spoke of the recent attacks, apprehension was evident in their voices. Curtis, on the other hand, talked almost boastfully about the way the killer snuck in under cover of darkness, undetected, and left such a bloody crime scene.

"There must be a clue," he said to the store clerk at the grocery store. "No one could commit such a brutal act and not leave a trace."

Kaylee looked at his hands and noticed the scratches. What were they from?

Everywhere they went, they couldn't escape it. The television in the restaurant where they stopped for lunch was tuned to the midday news.

"The recent murders have the police baffled and the community on edge," the reporter said.

Kaylee studied his face as they ate their lunch. Was Curtis the one? Was he the one that had wreaked havoc on this community? It was a peaceful mountain town until he came. Now it was anything but peaceful. Perhaps he was so comfortable with death that this didn't disturb him. But maybe, just maybe, the truth was closer than she realized.

"Let's get back to the cabin." Kaylee wiped her face with the napkin. "I think we've had enough talk of the killings for a while."

"Agreed." He motioned to the waitress for the check.

Kaylee buckled Stephanie into the car seat in the back of the Mustang and they headed up the mountain towards the cabin. Along the way, the traffic came to a stop.

"Wonder what's going on?" Curtis tried to see around the stopped traffic.

Frustrated, he got out and walked up ahead to a group standing on the side of the road.

"Seems like they found another body. Right along the road just up ahead," one man offered.

"I hope they find a suspect soon. This is really scary," a woman added

The sound of a helicopter filled the air.

"Do they think he is close by?" Curtis pointed to the helicopter in the sky. "Normally, they only send out the choppers to search when they think they are on the run."

"I hope not!" The lady's voice was noticeably shaking as she headed back to her car continually looking up at the circling helicopter.

Curtis looked around at the looks on the people's faces. He noticed the fear they all had. Did his face look the same? He did not feel fearful.

He furrowed his brow and parted his lips slightly, trying to mimic the looks he saw on their faces. It felt unnatural and foreign to him. Maybe psychopaths really were incapable of empathy. Had he merely pretended all his life to be charming and loving? He did not understand guilt. People had tried to explain it to him, but it never made any sense. But fear he had felt before. He remembered being scared of monsters hiding under his bed as a child. Pappy would say, "No need to be scared of monsters hiding under the bed, boy. The real monsters are hiding inside us."

Curtis brought himself back to those times when he would lay in his bed at night thinking of the monsters that hid deep inside him. This frightened him. He hoped his face showed this emotion.

Exhausted and tired of playing games, he headed back to the car.

"Seems they found another body. Must be fresh as they brought out the chopper." He buckled his seatbelt.

A police officer came up to the window on Curtis's side.

"Sir. We have an active investigation ahead and have closed the road. We ask that you turn around and take the detour. Officers are in place to direct you."

Curtis turned the car around and followed the slow line of traffic back around the mountain. After over an hour, they finally pulled into the driveway of the cabin. Kaylee was silent the whole way. There must be a lot on her mind.

"I'm going to put Steph down for a nap." She picked her up and headed to her room. "I think I'll lie down for a bit as well."

She didn't wait for an answer, and Curtis wasn't in the mood for conversation anyway. His killings had gotten out of hand. He was going out several times a week. They had only found five, now six of the bodies. He had killed twice a week, so there were four others yet to be discovered.

Maybe he should take Tucker for a walk and go "discover" one himself. It might be fun to be the good samaritan that called in one of his own kills. This time, he couldn't claim self-defense. He thought better of it. Maybe another day. Kaylee was on edge, and he needed to ensure his homelife was in balance.

The lines between his worlds were blurred. There wasn't any real distinction anymore. His behavior was sloppy. He knew his skin was under the fingernails of several of the victims. His blood was also at the crime scene. He couldn't chance the risk of his DNA, fingerprints, or blood being taken, as that would be his downfall. He didn't know how many murders he would be tied to. He had killed for almost fifteen years. There were hundreds of bodies scattered across the southern United States. If they found him, he would surely be put to death. He was without a doubt the most prolific serial killer that ever lived. This was a secret he would take to his grave, if he had anything to say about it.

———◆———●———◆———

Kaylee fell asleep as soon as her head touched the pillow. The thoughts of Curtis killing all those innocent people were too much for her to bear. Her subconscious worked through the details as she slept.

The scene of the aberrations swirled in her head. It always started the same. The line of people walking from the forest across the field of grass as the fog cleared. The fire they headed towards was off in the distance. She saw the man with the serpent tattoo near the fire. There were so many victims. Kaylee struggled each time to find clues in their faces.

Suddenly, she saw Pappy. He stood at the edge of the trees. His mouth moved, but she couldn't hear anything. She kept saying, "I can't hear you, Pappy. What did you say?"

She tried to move closer to him, but she couldn't. She strained her eyes to read his lips. The wind began to howl, and suddenly they were side by side in a clearing in a forest. Pappy had the gash on his head, and his arm hung broken by his side.

"Pappy. I'm so sorry we couldn't save you that day."

"Kaylee, that's not important. I am okay now."

"I don't know what to do," she whispered.

"Madness runs through his bloodline. The version of him you fell in love with no longer exists. You are not safe. They will keep coming. Take the little one. She does not belong in his world."

"I miss the old times. The happy times. Everything has changed."

"It is his road and his alone. You can walk with him, but you can't walk it for him. He has reached a level of darkness from which many don't return. He is strong; stronger than most. Hopefully, he will come out the other side and find his way back to you. It is a path he must travel alone."

The wind started to blow, and Kaylee was surrounded by dense fog so thick she couldn't see her hand in front of her face.

"Pappy? Pappy, are you still there?"

Kaylee suddenly woke drenched in sweat, her face wet with tears. She understood Pappy's message. Was she strong enough to follow it?

~ CHAPTER 14 ~
Final Shot

Something inside him mutated. As the weeks turned to months, Curtis continued to spiral out of control. Freedom and power fueled the fire within. The hellfire he fueled was set to engulf everything in its path. It didn't matter. He was brazen and bold, untouchable.

The killings were all people talked about. It was all around him. The more the fire was fanned, the hotter it burned, and the more brazen he became. It was his legacy. He wanted to become a legend because of it, but he could not take credit for it. Not yet. To do so would require being caught. That was the epic final battle. No one in the Mason bloodline had ever been caught. Curtis knew he would not be the first.

"I'm headed out to town to pick up some glue to fix the loose chairs." He grabbed his keys and slid them into his pocket. "Need me to pick anything up?"

"I can't think of anything." Kaylee sat at her computer working on another freelance article for the local paper. "I'm almost finished with this piece. Then I was planning to take a walk with Stephanie and Tucker. The last of the summer flowers are blooming, and I wanted to get some cuttings for us to make some arrangements and wreaths."

"Stephanie would love that." He headed out the door.

"See ya!" she called as the screen door of the cabin slammed shut, marking his departure.

The brightness of the late morning sun caused him to squint. He grabbed his sunglasses from the visor of the Mustang and caught his reflection in the rearview mirror. Looking back while going forward. That was a mantra he could sink his teeth into. He smiled at himself. He had the kind of face that stopped people in their tracks. The sand-rough stubble that covered his lower cheeks and chin amplified his rugged masculine appearance. People always remarked that his entrancing mariner-blue eyes were his best feature. They were spellbinding and bewitched all those who fell under his steady gaze. Even with them obscured by the dark glasses, he still radiated energy, purpose, and authority. He lowered his glasses, continuing to stare at his reflection. He winked and raised his eyebrow as he lowered the shades back over his eyes.

The drive to the town was uneventful. He went about his errand and gathered the needed supplies and started back up the mountain towards the cabin. As he approached the entrance to the scenic parkway of the Blue Ridge Mountains, he decided to take a short ride. His mother always loved the mountain flowers. He felt a need to experience them. Maybe it was her spirit that drew him; maybe it was something else.

As he turned onto the winding, two-lane road, he rolled down the window and breathed deeply. The mountain air filled his lungs and warmed his heart. His family roots were deeply planted in the mountains. He was the last of his bloodline, he and Stephanie. Would she inherit the Mason family ways? A part of him wished it carried on through her; another part hoped it died with him.

Everyone he loved had been taken from him. With each passing, a piece of his soul died with them to a point where there was nothing left. Kaylee had brought some light into the dark, shadowy pit in which he wallowed. The evil that stirred within him was too strong. Deep-seated and engrained in his psyche. The two could not be separated. There was no cure for what ailed him. There was no magic pill, potion, or spell that could deter him from his predestined course.

That day, on that mountain road, beside the low wooden guardrail, Curtis succumbed to the demon within. The full power of the evil that was caged within him for thirty years erupted as the Mustang broke free from the confines of the road.

His foot never left the accelerator as the red blur flew over the rail and into the air as the ground cut sharply away. The engine roared, the back wheels spun widely as the car carried him through the air. It wasn't the flight, it was the landing he dreaded.

Like something out of a movie, the car glided as the back tires got closer to the ground. They touched and hurled the car forward as the trees branches were sheared off and the car plowed a path of destruction. His hands gripped the steering wheel tighter, his arms straight as he braced for an impact that never really came.

The windshield shattered as the Mustang came to rest in the brush on the side of the mountain. Astonished that he was not hurt, he surveyed the damage. The Mustang was beyond repair, but he didn't have a scratch. He was invincible!

The strong smell of gasoline filled his nose as he walked away from the car that he had gotten when he was sixteen. They had been through so much. It had carried his mother, his wife, his daughter, his grandparents—not to mention countless victims. It served him well over the years. It was time to move on. It no longer fit his purpose. It represented a life he was no longer a part of. He reached into his pocket and pulled out a book of matches. There was one left.

How fitting. He ripped it off the paper book and struck it against the flint strip on the back. It flared, and he threw it over his shoulder like salt after a spill. He never looked back as he felt the heat erupt as the fuel caught fire. He was a distance away when the explosion ripped through the countryside.

Suddenly, he realized he wasn't alone.

A woman appeared before him from the trees. "Did you hear that explosion?" She was visibly shaken.

"There was a car wreck. A car flew off the parkway just over there. Probably something sparked the gas." He paused only briefly as he offered the explanation.

"Do you think anyone's hurt?" Her voice was still shaking.

"I don't know."

He was annoyed that she kept talking to him. He stopped, turned, and looked at her. There was something about her. What was her story? Why did their paths cross? Why now? Curtis believed the Universe gave you what you need. Why did he need this scared woman? Suddenly, he realized. She needed him, not the other way around.

He reached up and smoothed out his disheveled hair. His sunglasses were still on. He popped them up on top of his head. She looked in his eyes, hypnotized. He tilted his head to the side and examined her face. He raised his arm and struck her upside her face with the back of his hand.

She fell backwards to the ground as she rubbed her cheek with her hand. Curtis saw the bruise as it started to form. He stepped quickly towards her as she crawled backwards away from his advances. He looked around and picked up a large stick and swung it at her head. As it connected, he saw the blood and heard her skull crush under his powerful blows. Her screams of terror echoed in his head, but he didn't care. The demons had taken over and they feasted on blood. With each scream, he gained power. He swung the stick until she stopped moving and was silent.

He threw the stick on top of her and walked away pleased with his accomplishment.

He didn't hear them as they approached. He felt the sting in his side. He reached down thinking a bee had stung him. He was shocked when he looked at his hand and it was covered in blood. He raised his shirt. He had been shot. He heard another shot ring off nearby. He ran.

Someone had seen him. He had been careless. He couldn't get caught. This kill wasn't planned. It was random and opportunistic. He tripped up. He knew he needed to get to Kaylee. She would help him. He wished Pappy was still alive.

He had enough sense to stop the blood from dripping. He wasn't going to give them a trail to follow. He took off his shirt and wrapped it around his torso.

———————•———————

Kaylee stopped suddenly in the woods and grabbed Stephanie's hand. «We need to grab the last few flowers and head back home," she said with an even, calm tone.

She was anything but calm. Something bad had happened. She heard the explosion, sirens, and then gunshots a short time later. What if he was caught? The only thing worse than raising her daughter with a secret serial killer was the world knowing his identity. She could never let that happen.

They cut the final stems then placed them in the basket and walked purposefully back to the cabin. They had just entered the kitchen when Kaylee saw him at the edge of the woods. Even from the distance she could tell he was disoriented. She opened the back door, and their eyes met.

He didn't have a shirt. Something was tied around his middle and it looked like he was injured. His hand cradled his side, and he was slightly bent over. Still, he walked with purpose.

"Let's get you inside." Kaylee moved his hand and saw the blood. "What happened?"

He leaned on her as she maneuvered him to the wobbly kitchen chair he'd planned to fix. The irony of the situation didn't go unnoticed. If it chose this moment to break, that would be fitting.

She shook the idea from her head as she focused on Curtis.

"I wrecked the Mustang. Ran it off the side of the parkway. I wasn't hurt, so I started walking." He winced as Kaylee poured alcohol on the wound to clean it out. "I heard the explosion. Guess there was a gas leak."

"So what about this?" She pointed to the gunshot wound on his side.

"That? An unexpected complication, you could say."

She looked at him. He wasn't going to say. It would come out soon enough.

"I think it's still inside." She looked at his back. "There isn't an exit wound. It will have to come out."

"We can't go to the hospital, Kaylee."

"I have an idea." She picked up the phone and dialed the familiar number. She explained that Curtis had got into some trouble and needed medical help.

"Someone's coming." She hung up the phone.

"Your friend?"

"Not him. But he will send someone."

Kaylee intentionally did not tell Curtis about Rupert. Some things were best kept secret. He was her only true confidant. He was always just a call away.

The doctor showed up about an hour later, removed the bullet, and stitched Curtis up. He left some painkillers and antibiotics and said Curtis should be fine in a week or so.

That night after she gave Curtis his dose of meds, Kaylee picked up the phone.

"Rupert, I can't keep this up." Her sobs radiated through the phone. "This is the hardest thing I have ever done. I don't know if I can make it alone."

"Just because the decision cuts deeply doesn't mean it's wrong."

"I know." She wiped the tears from her cheek.

"Ten years from now, make sure you can say that you chose your life. You didn't settle. You have the courage."

"It's so hard to walk away from someone you love way too much."

"But walk away you must."

"I know." She let the words fill the silence for a while.

"I'll put things in order," Rupert said in a quiet, solemn tone. "Give me a few days."

"We need to disappear. Kaylee Smith-Roberts cannot exist and neither can Stephanie."

"I will make it so."

As she hung up the phone, a sense of peace flooded over her. She had forgotten what it felt like, having lived in fear for so long. She had made the right decision. The voices in her head echoed in unison: *We are proud.*

She checked on Stephanie.

"Good night, sweet princess." She straightened the covers as Tucker wagged his tail. Tucker always slept with her.

Kaylee went to her room and climbed into bed next to Curtis. This was one of the last nights she would fall asleep to the sound of his breathing. She would miss that. It always brought her a sense of security. Kaylee knew Curtis would die for her and Stephanie. She also knew they weren't going to die for him.

Kaylee woke before the sun. There was a lot on her mind. She needed to make Curtis understand. She knew the cops would be all over the farm back home. They had found his car. There was nothing linking her name with the cabin. She had used one of her pseudonyms for her freelance work.

She sat at the kitchen table and held the hot cup of steaming coffee when Curtis came in. He still wasn't moving very well. He poured himself a cup of coffee and lowered himself into a chair. His face showed the pain he felt.

"I'll get you some more pain meds." She got up and grabbed the bottle off the counter and handed him two pills.

He popped them into his mouth and washed them down with the steaming liquid.

They sat silently for a while. The words that needed to be said weighed heavily on her heart. How could she crush the one man that truly loved her? He was in no shape to take care of himself. *Stop making excuses.* Procrastination would not benefit anyone.

Curtis broke the silence first. "Just spit it out."

She jerked her head up at his words.

"We both know the conversation that needs to be discussed, so just rip that bandage off. Neither of us are known to back away from a difficult situation."

"I know what needs to happen, but it's not what I want." Tears welled in her eyes.

He reached across the table and placed his hand over hers.

His touch shot fire through her to her very soul.

"Do you have a plan?"

"I'm working on it. Rupert is pulling something together for us."

Curtis nodded as he took another sip. "It's the right thing. We both know that." He squeezed her hand. "When no one is watching. When they can't see what I am doing or thinking. That is when my true colors show. The eyes of the devil look at me in the mirror. I have gone to a level of hell that you can't even fathom. I am fighting devils so powerful it would destroy you. I know you must go."

He always knew what she needed to hear, how to support her in just the right way.

After everything that had happened, they both knew the only option was for Kaylee to raise Stephanie alone. There would always be another person hunting him, trying to use them to get at Curtis. It wasn't fair for Stephanie, and she deserved a chance to live, not simply survive.

"Perhaps one day we'll meet again as characters in a different story. Maybe then our ending will be different." She walked around the table and kissed him deeply.

Over the next few days, Curtis regained his strength. They spent time as a family, made memories that would need to last a lifetime. Kaylee wasn't sure how she would explain it to Stephanie.

A few days later, Rupert called. He had everything ready. He had arranged for someone to watch after

Curtis until he could return to the farm. He dropped by the next day.

Kaylee had loaded everything into the silver Civic. Rupert had dropped off a tan Altima for Curtis. He had taken care of reporting his Mustang stolen to disconnect Curtis from anything here. Curtis had Rupert transfer money into an account so Kaylee and Stephanie would never have to want for anything.

They stood at the door and looked at each other. Goodbyes were always the hardest. She reached out, kissed him. He held on like he never wanted to let go.

"I love you, Mommy and Daddy!" Stephanie wrapped her arms around their legs. "Are we ready for our adventure?"

Kaylee nodded.

"We will see you when the road decides it's time for our paths to cross again." Kaylee took Stephanie's hand and walked away.

~ CHAPTER 15 ~
Sharp Edges

That morning, she woke up different. She wouldn't stay broken forever. She picked up the pieces and weaved them back together. Only this time, the sharp edges were showing. They had started over. Kaylee returned to Chicago, Illinois. It wasn't the same as when she left. She wasn't the same. She would build a life for her and Stephanie. It was easy to get lost in the big city.

Rupert had set them up with new identities. They kept their first names, but their last name was simply Roberts. Kaylee used the name K.S. Roberts for her writing along with several other pen names. They thought it would be easier for Stephanie if they didn't change things too drastically.

She got an apartment downtown on the north side of town. There was a park on the Chicago River just outside their building. It was perfect for Tucker. Kaylee stayed busy writing. Stephanie started preschool. They made friends and started to finally enjoy life. Kaylee had almost forgotten what it was like before. Things were simple, predictable, peaceful. She liked it. The visions that came to her at night had calmed. She hadn't had any since she left Curtis. Somewhere deep inside there was a piece of her heart that longed for him. It always would.

"Perhaps writing the obituary for Kaylee Smith-Roberts would get it out of my head." Kaylee still talked to herself as she worked through things.

"Maybe more of an ode rather than an obituary. There has been so much death. I am still very much alive and have fought to stay that way." She laughed at the thought of what her headline would say. "Broken woman falls in love with deranged killer, live at five."

She sat down in front of the computer, her hands poised over the keyboard. She took two deep breaths and started to type. The words raced from her head to her fingers as they filled page after page. Her life story in black and white. It was cathartic. It was the cleansing she needed to rid her conscience of the vile memories that cut deep. As she wrote, she realized one had to go through something that destroyed them in order to realize who they were meant to become, who they truly were.

Curtis was a part of her as she was of him. That was the way it was supposed to be. The way the Universe wanted it to be. She embraced this and she thrived.

Ode to Demons

Raven hair and witchlike eyes, a life of pain she did endure.

The devil she saw would haunt her so, the sprits calmed her mortal soul.

She led a life where stories told, her inner fears and thoughts of bold

Evil lurked within her world. Kill she did to protect her own.

The man she loved was a feat of strength, a stone pillar behind a wall.

A fortress too high for most to climb, she scaled the height to see inside.

A place where demons danced and souls died, the horror and blood cut to her core.

There was no way to even the score; he killed for pleasure to end one's pain.

She wanted to believe that she could gain the trust, the love of the monster inside.

The beast within him, it must die.

She cut him with love and gave him a child; the crazy inside him could not hide.

The man that she loved, he died on that mountain; the man that stood now was no one she knew.

She looked at their child and knew her way out, was one that would require she never look back.

She left him behind with the blood and the death, a new path she forged one steeped in regret.

She had walked through hell with a presence so bold; she stared death in the face her truth must be told.

To the city of wind she lived in the sky; where she started this journey is where it would die.

She built a life filled with joy and hope, total immersion as the cure it would lend.

She knew he was out there but couldn't be seen, haunted by souls of people he killed.

He never left her side, he lived in her mind; their paths they would cross, a future to hold.

The Universe would beacon their story be told.

She leaned back, read, and reread the lines. The self-doubt crept back and she shook her head. It was awful. She was a hot mess and so was this ode. She saved it under "Works in Progress."

~ CHAPTER 16 ~
KRISTI REVISITED

The loneliness he felt couldn't be filled by just any company. What he sought was a closeness, to be needed by someone. As Curtis adjusted to his life without Kaylee and Stephanie, he wasn't ready for the isolation he felt. He was healed from his injury, and it was time for him to return to the plantation. Before he did that, he wanted to revisit one final loose end that needed to be tidied up.

He picked up the phone, and without hesitation he dialed the number.

"Hello?" A familiar voice on the other end answered.

"Hi Kristi, this is Curtis MacIntyre," he said with a smile in his voice.

"Curtis?" Kristi paused for a moment before continuing. "What a surprise hearing from you. How have you been?"

"Pretty good. I'm going to be in town for a while and thought maybe we could catch up."

"I guess that would be okay. What did you have in mind?"

"Maybe an early dinner? I'm driving back from the mountains today and should be in town late afternoon." Curtis shifted the phone around.

"Sounds good. Why don't we meet at that barbecue place around four or so?"

"Perfect." Curtis was excited to see Kristi again and have a chance to catch up. "See you then."

A little while later, Curtis was on the road. As he left the crisp air of the mountains behind, he was excited for what lay down the road. This was his new beginning, and he was determined not to repeat his mistakes. He would be smarter this time. Pappy was right in not confiding in Grandma about the "family business."

He pulled into the parking lot of the restaurant and saw Kristi waiting on a bench outside. He parked and walked over to her. There was a young girl with her. She had blonde, curly hair and looked to be a little older than Stephanie. Kristi had told him she didn't have any children back in the hospital when Stephanie was born.

"Hi." Curtis approached the bench. "I see you brought a friend."

"This is Genevieve." She touched the girl's curls.

The little girl snuggled in close to Kristi.

"Genevieve, this is Mr. MacIntyre, a friend of mine."

"Nice to meet you." Curtis crouched down so he was at her eye level. "I have a little girl that's pretty close to your age."

"I am four and a half." She held up four fingers on one hand and bent her pointer finger on the other signifying the half year.

"You most certainly are." Kristi laughed at the precision in which she communicated her age. "That half year is important."

"My little girl is this many." He held up his fingers.

"Three and a half!" she squealed counting his fingers as she wiggled on the bench.

"That's right!" With a big smile, he tried to put the young child at ease.

"Can we go eat? I'm a little bit hungry." Genevieve let go of her mother's arm and inched towards the edge of the bench.

"Most certainly." Curtis motioned for them to lead the way as he fell in behind the two ladies.

As they looked at the menu, they talked about Kristi's nursing career and Curtis going back on the road. Genevieve played contently with the condiment containers on the table. Meticulously, she stacked the individual butter tubs interspersed with sugar packets like building blocks. Her structure proved quite dramatic.

The waitress brought their food, and they each enjoyed what they'd chosen.

"Mommy?" Genevieve looked towards Kristi. "Can I try a bite of yours?"

"Sure, Gen." Kristi casually filled her fork with a small bite and handed it to Genevieve.

It seemed very natural. There was no hesitation. This child was Kristi's. What would cause her to be secretive? He started to do the math in his head.

She was about fifteen to eighteen months older than Stephanie. Could it be? Did he have another child? Curtis remained silent on the paternal connection, and they continued to enjoy the meal.

He lingered longer than normal with Kristi and Genevieve. Genevieve was a very intelligent child. She seemed advanced for her age. He soaked up every detail of the little girl's face, her mannerisms, the sound of her laugh. The curly hair was not from his side; that was from Kristi. Her intelligence, that was clearly from him. He smiled.

"What are you thinking about?" Kristi interrupted his thoughts.

"Nothing really." He turned his eyes from Genevieve. The way the gold color radiated through her blue eyes, that was from him. Did Kristi know that?

"Your eyes are so pretty," Curtis said to Genevieve, although it was more directed towards Kristi.

"The color is quite rare." Kristi smiled as she straightened her posture and leaned forward towards him.

Curtis furrowed his brow. "Are they blue or green?"

"Technically, they are blue and yellow," Kristi answered as she explained the heterochromatic coloring of her eyes.

"The way the gold dances through them is very unusual." He examined Kristi's eyes. "You don't have that."

"No." Kristi opened her eyes wider.

"Is it genetic?" He felt she was his. This would tell him the answer he sought. He held his breath as he waited for the response.

"Yes." Spoken so quietly that even the ghosts of his victims couldn't hear.

"Where does it come from if it's genetic?" He already knew the answer.

"It comes from her father." Kristi finished the food on her plate and laid her silverware across the edge.

Curtis understood she was done with this line of questioning, and it was time to move on or she would. He let Kristi hold onto her secret for now, even though they both knew the truth.

Curtis found himself, once again, trying to squeeze a lifetime of memories into a few hours. The irony did not go unnoticed. His demons had already cost him one child and the woman he loved. He couldn't risk a second. Pappy's words came to the forefront of his mind: "Grandma knows nothing and never will. She would not understand. The guilt would be more than she could bear. Thus, she never can know." Kristi would be the same. She could never see the killer behind his mask.

The waitress came back to the table several times after they paid the check. Her increased annoyance was evident in her voice.

"Are you sure you don't want anything else?" she snapped with her hand perched on her hip.

With a genuine smile on his face, Curtis joyfully replied, "No ma'am. We were just leaving."

"Have a nice day." She picked up the remaining glasses from the table as they gathered their things.

The bright sun slapped them in their faces as they exited the restaurant.

"If you have some time, perhaps you would like to hang out a bit longer. My house is not far from here, and there is a pool if Genevieve would like to splash around a bit."

"Oh, Mommy! Can we? Please? Please?"

"I think we can swing by for a bit." Kristi squeezed her daughter's hand as she reached out and gently touched Curtis's arm with the other.

<hr />

Curtis secretly wished he could see the look on Genevieve's face when she saw the MacIntyre Estate for the first time. The two cars descended upon the stone wall that marked the property as they headed down the road towards the entry gate. The sound of the turn signal in his car punctuated the passage to the next phase of his life. One that would allow him to share a piece of himself with Kristi and their child.

He slowed and turned into the drive as the strong metal gates swung open allowing them entrance into his world. The world he allowed the public to see. The cars made their way to the grand portico.

Curtis expected the sound of Tucker's bellow to come from the front porch as he jumped off the chair, stretched, and trotted to the edge of the stone porch. Curtis opened his car door and stopped himself before he called for the hound.

Kaylee had taken Tucker with them. The house appeared eerily quiet.

One of the old barn cats walked up to them. "This is one of our barn cats. We call him Sir Fluff. He normally just hangs out in the barn." Curtis reached down to stroke its fur.

"Hi, Sir Fluff." Genevieve wrapped her arms around his neck and gave him a big hug.

Curtis chuckled a little as his offspring went straight for the cat's neck. Would the Mason genetics rear its ugly head in the next generation?

Fluff responded with a loud purr and a butt on her chin once he was freed from her grip. The little girl giggled.

"Shall we?" Curtis pointed towards the front door

"This is not what we expected."

"I get that a lot." Curtis took Kristi's hand as he led them into the house.

Curtis showed them around the house as he pointed out the pool table, library, and pool in the basement. He was happy when Genevieve preferred to go out back to see the gardens and the cows. He walked them through his mother's gardens as he pointed out her favorite flowers.

"Mom always loved roses and lavender." Curtis pulled out a small pocketknife from his pocket as he looked over the pink roses.

"Here's a nice one." He clipped the bloom, cleared the stem of thorns, and handed it to Genevieve. "The pink ones were her favorite."

Genevieve eagerly took the flower and sniffed it. "It smells pretty!"

Kristi smiled at her as they continued the walk through the gardens.

Memories are strongest when they relate to several senses. The smell of roses hopefully would remind Genevieve of her day at the plantation with him.

They entered the cool shade of the barn. Genevieve, still grasping her flower tight, ran over to the stalls and looked between the slats.

"Where are the animals?" Her nose crinkled up and her brow furrowed at the disappointment.

"They are all in the fields. We let them run around in the grass most of the time." Curtis went over and picked her up so she could see into the stall better. "Would you like to go on a hayride and try to find them?"

"Can we, Mommy?"

"Of course, sweetie." Kristi laughed. "Curtis, you are full of all sorts of secrets."

"You have no idea, babe."

Curtis got the tractor hitched up to the wagon and piled in a few hay bales as Kristi and Genevieve looked around the barn. Déjà vu. This scene had played out before with Stephanie and Kaylee. What were the chances that both his children would ride in the wagon around the farm? What was the chance that he would actually have two daughters?

"All aboard for the hayride," Curtis called out.

Genevieve ran towards him as her flower swung wildly in her tightly clutched fist. She scampered up the ladder and took her place right in the front behind the tractor.

"Come on, Mommy. Hurry up!" she demanded. "We have to find the cows."

They headed off through the gate into the fields in search of the ever-elusive cow herd. They spent the afternoon riding around the farm. Curtis stopped so that Kristi and Genevieve could jump out and see the cows. They found several calves with their mothers. Genevieve hugged each one of them.

He was amazed at the love that poured from this little girl. Her spirit was so joyful and caring. She reminded him so much of his mother and her ability to spread love and to see the beauty in the world. Genevieve had this ability as well. Good or bad, she shared his lifeblood.

The conversation with Kristi needed to happen. How to broach the subject was the question. It needed to happen today, but not in front of Genevieve. Patience would be his friend. He needed to wait for the right time.

As the afternoon sun crept low in the sky, Genevieve grew tired. She found a spot under the large willow tree in the back and lay down with Sir Fluff by her side. Her hand stroked the barn cat's orange fur as she sung to him quietly.

"What is she singing?" Curtis didn't recognize the songs.

"She makes them up." Kristi walked over towards the chairs on the porch.

Curtis got some iced tea from the refrigerator just inside the back door and poured them each a glass.

"She is quite creative."

Kristi nodded in agreement as she took a sip of the cold drink. "Thanks. This is just what I needed." She motioned to the glass of iced tea.

They both sat silently.

"Kristi, I'm not sure how to bring this up." The ice clanked in his glass as he swirled it nervously. "So I'll just say it straight up."

Kristi put her glass down and folded her hands in her lap.

"Is she mine?"

His words cut through the air like a knife through flesh. The core of its meaning exposed to the world. To be judged harshly. Unfavorably. He stared at her face and scanned her body as he read every silent word it screamed at him.

Her eyelids were shut. Her head bowed as if in prayer. The fingers on her hands restless as she tried in vain to brush off the reality of the conversation he started. His knees bounced, and her shoulders shook as she slowly raised her head and her eyes opened.

That initial spark that flew from them told him she was a force to be reckoned with. She was fierce and would protect her child at any cost. Curtis knew that look. He had seen it before. Several times. Kaylee had that look when she left. He had seen it in his own reflection in the eyes of the Serpent. It was powerful. He would not challenge her. There was no need.

"Yes." Her voice was level. The word was stern and powerful. She stood her ground and marked her territory simultaneously. Her body sat motionless in the chair. Her eyes locked on his. His mastery of body language helped him navigate. She was ready to fight if needed. So was he. Was there a need?

They both remained unmoving. Each unwilling to back down. This was a battle neither would surrender. The stakes were too great. The war is lost due to miscalculations unfolding. Curtis knew the two most powerful attributes of a warrior were patience and time. He had plenty of both.

He continued to read and respond to her cues. He let her lead this dance. She unclenched her hands and laid her palms face down on her thighs. He knew it was time to strike.

"I will provide for her." The words meant to comfort and reassure Kristi.

"What?" Her eyebrows raised in surprise at his words. "We never want for anything. I promise you that."

"I know." He lowered his eyes. "I would be honored to share what I have with you both. To provide a safety net for you both. You can just keep it for a rainy day."

Kristi's eyes narrowed as she stared at him.

He knew she was calculating the risk. Did he succeed in convincing her his intentions were genuine? Empathy was not his strength, after all he was a prolific serial killer. He puffed out his chest unconsciously.

Suspicion crossed her face. "I'm not sure that's a good idea."

He quickly rounded his shoulders and resumed a submissive posture, but it was too late. The damage was done, and she was an astute opponent.

"Let me at least set up an account in your name. You will have complete control and can do with it as you see fit. You can even donate it to a charity if you want." Curtis stared at her sheepishly.

"You aren't going to give up, are you?" Kristi sat back in the chair. "Fine. I'll send you the information on where to transfer the money."

Curtis sat back and smiled. He had won.

"*In omnia paratus.*" Kristi whispered.

"What?" Curtis leaned forward. "That's Latin."

"Yes. *Ready for anything* is the translation," she countered. "It's my life's motto."

Curtis's mouth dropped open as Kristi picked up her iced tea and took a long drink.

She was a strong woman who could take care of herself. Maybe he didn't win after all? Maybe, just maybe, he had fallen under her spell and she was calling the shots.

~ CHAPTER 17 ~

Two Lone Wolves

The days he spent with Kristi and Genevieve weighed heavy on his mind. He had arranged to transfer several million dollars to the account Kristi had provided. He would never see them again. All that girl would have was great memories of a fun day on the farm with one of her mother's friends. Could he truly stay away? Time would tell.

When you walk through hell, do so like you own the place. He had survived a new level of hell and had come out the other side changed. His focus was now on creating his future.

The familiar stone fence came up on the right side of the road. Home sweet home. There wasn't much sweet about it anymore. It was a constant reminder of what might have been. Dreams crushed to dust by his own hands. He turned down the drive in the bland, nondescript Altima that Rupert had arranged for him. It certainly wasn't his Mustang.

He saw the house for the first time through new eyes. The worn facade showed years of neglect. Paint peeled at the top of the portico where the columns met the roof. The limestone steps showed wear. Chips and cracks were everywhere. The bushes were in dire need of a trim, and the driveway needed a fresh top dressing of crushed stone.

Maybe it was time to sell the place. He walked up the stairs and laid his hand on the black cast-iron door handle. It felt rough and cold like his heart. He gripped it tightly. It was firm and strong. It had weathered many storms and come out the other side with some wear but relatively unscathed. Functional. It served its purpose. It was the gatekeeper to his world. It kept out the intruders. It served as the passageway for those he let close. Both his children and their mothers had laid hands on this knob. It held a sacred place in his soul.

He pulled his shirt out and polished the dark metal. The cotton T-shirt buffed it as he rubbed off years of neglect, abandonment, and loneliness. That handle had stood on that door for his entire life. He never paused to admire its simple beauty. He was glad he took the time. He pushed the lever down with his thumb. He felt the indentation in the metal. It fit him perfectly, like an old pair of boots.

He chuckled as he pushed the door open and announced, "I'm home."

The house was eerily quiet. He heard the sound of his own heartbeat as it pounded in his head. He dropped his bag at the bottom of the stairs. The house was spotless. The cleaners had continued to come weekly even while no one was there. He walked back to the kitchen and opened the refrigerator, surprised it was stocked with food. Someone must have tipped them off that he was coming home.

He glanced out the window. Something caught his attention. A wolf in the field stared directly at him. He watched it for a while as it walked about surveying its territory. Deciding to get a closer look, he went out on the back patio and sat down, quietly so as not to disturb the animal. He rocked slowly in the chair, softly so the springs didn't squeak.

Still, the animal heard it. Its ears perked up as it turned in his direction. It started to walk towards him, gradually increasing its speed. As it trotted toward the house, Curtis noticed the toned muscles under its fur. How effortlessly it moved as it glided through the grass. It was a marvel to behold. Like him, an athlete.

It slowed, cautiously guarded as it approached the steps. It was a stunning creature. She exuded a quiet confidence that screamed so loudly it could not be ignored. Curtis appreciated that. Her coat was pure white with hints of silver at the end of the hairs. Her bushy tail waved slowly back and forth as she stared directly into his eyes. She waited, unwavering in her commitment. She had mastered the art of knowing when to be aggressive and when to stay patient. He wished he had that skill.

The pain she had endured showed in her eyes. Scars of heroic battles showed in her coat. There was a magic about her. He continued to stare in her golden eyes, and he found his soul. She was a mighty warrior, silent until she needed to fight. She fought with a ferocity that few possessed. Curtis understood.

He tipped his head to the side and lowered his eyes. She responded with the same and started up the steps. She approached his chair as he remained motionless. Her nose twitched as she picked up his scent. Her lips parted as her teeth touched the skin on his hand. She paused and licked him gently.

He reached over and rubbed her scruff. She let him. He felt the muscles ripple under his hand. She was powerful, a mighty hunter, just like him. They sat on the porch for hours that day. When Curtis got up to head inside, he was surprised when she followed him through the door.

She made herself at home, and he decided to let her stay. He called her Aspen. She kept him company and made the house less lonely. She followed him as he went about the mindless hours of maintenance the house so desperately craved. She watched. It was as if she could read his mind too, like Kaylee.

◆────────●────────◆

Curtis craved the open road. He was never one to stay at home for long. He had arranged to drive for Hughes Trucking again. The familiar routine would do him some good. He climbed aboard his blue rig. The air seat swished as he lowered his weight into it. He pulled on the air horn as he passed through the gate.

His window was down as always. The wind whipped through his hair as he looked over at Aspen. She sat tall in the seat beside him, her nose pointed toward her window as she breathed in the exotic scents of the open road.

"Are you ready for our next adventure, girl?" he asked as he scratched her behind her bushy ears. "Thought maybe we could do a little hunting along the way. I think you would like the fresh meat."

Curtis's eyes sparkled as he talked to his wolf dog. She turned her head towards him, the corners of her mouth curving upwards in the semblance of a smile.

"We are going to make quite the team. Yes we are." They drove down the road to nowhere.

Note from the Author

Road to Nowhere came to life serendipitously as the second book in the Driven to Kill series. I decided that I would break my first fiction book into a trilogy, and Book 1, *Down the Road,* was off to the editor, so I focused on the next leg of the story. As I continued thinking about Curtis and Kaylee's story, I wanted it to span generations. I plotted and outlined scenes of their children and what their life was like being the offspring of a prolific serial killer who continued to evade capture.

As I continued with the story line, it became apparent that there was a large time gap between the two books, thus I decided to put the draft, plots, and outline that I had been working on aside and save them for book 3. Alas, *Road to Nowhere* was born.

This story focused on Kaylee as a new mother and the struggles she faced as she balanced her maternal instincts to protect her child and her personal desires to be with the man she loved. This story captures Kaylee as she comes to terms with what ultimately we all know must be done. Most mothers will know which won out. I often told my husband, Tom, over the years, that if it came down to choosing between him and our daughter, she would come first every time. Something transforms inside when you become a parent. It is the perfect balance of absolute exhilaration punctuated with pure terror. The responsibility for another life is a tremendous and epic honor.

When I was in my mid-twenties, I was told by my doctor that I would not be able to conceive a child. That was the inciting moment that started a five-year journey to overcome my infertility. After the line of six positive pregnancy tests, the reality finally sank in; we were going to be parents. Our friends and family who walked that journey with us, when the odds were stacked against us, know the elation we felt when Casey finally made her appearance in the world. She was early, extremely small, but strong and quite the fighter. She is truly our greatest accomplishment.

The one thing I have learned through this process is that anything you dream can become reality as long as you put your mind to it. I hope that you enjoyed *Road to Nowhere*. There are several references to *Down the Road* Book 1 in the Driven to Kill series as well as breadcrumbs that may or may not appear in future books. Who is that guy with the serpent tattoo anyway, and why is he showing up in Kaylee's visions? Will he show up in the final book in the Driven to Kill series, *Road Back Home?* Stay tuned as we find out what happens with Stephanie and Genevieve as they go on their own epic journey searching for answers.

Acknowledgements

The encouragement of many have allowed the second book in the Driven to Kill series to come to life. The unwavering support of Casey and Tom, my family, and friends whose special gifts have inspired the characters and scenes written within this tale. Without the wisdom and guidance of my publishing team, this journey would not have happened. Morgan Gist MacDonald at the helm of Paper Raven Books and her incredible team of experts who worked tirelessly turning my vision and messy manuscript into perfect narrative prose and gripping scenes. Polishing my words until they unfolded into a story that immerses the reader and transports them into the fictional world of Kaylee and Curtis and their epic journey in search of love and acceptance. My editor and coach Jennifer Crosswhite of Tandem Services has truly transformed me from a novice to a published author, of multiple books.

This journey has been truly humbling and surreal. There have been so many that have a hand in making this book. My sister Valerie Short, who offered her expertise and gifted eye to guide the incredible talents of Zeppelin DG as he crafted the cover design. My friend Leah Parrish, who is always willing to go on adventures that inspire us both to live our best, authentic lives. My writer's group comrades from Writers on a Mission and the Get It Done: the Productive Writer's Group: Vera, Paula, Sandra, Ariel, Richardson, and Xan and others who shared the joint vision of creating a community of indie writers to work on their manuscripts while enduring a global pandemic, each making time to show up and make time to feed our passion for writing.

My story in my mind came to life on the pages of this book due to a community of diverse individuals who each brought their own talent and formed a circle of inspiration that envelops us all, individually and collectively. As I release *Road to Nowhere*, Book 2 of the Driven to Kill series, I am reminded of how far I have traveled as a writer, an artist, a creator. I look forward to continuing on this epic journey and completing Curtis and Kaylee's story. As in the end, as we follow our dreams, we all become stories. Make yours epic!

HERE IS A SNEAK PEEK OF BOOK 3

ROAD BACK HOME

~ CHAPTER 1 ~
Next Generation Family Business

The shadow of a tall, slender woman passed by the front window of the business in Philadelphia, Pennsylvania. The street was spattered with funeral homes like sprinkles on a child's birthday cake. Some right next to each other. Each with their own recognizable Italian heritage. The man watching from within noticed the shadow moving slowly as it approached the door that read Lorenzo Funeral Home.

Vincent Lorenzo knew that shadow well. It was that of his girlfriend, Stephanie Roberts. The familiar chimes announced her entrance. He looked up at the stunning beauty that stood before him. The reflection of the lights danced off her striking green eyes. He had only seen eyes like those one other time and that was on Stephanie's mother. Both of them had eyes that lit up a room and mesmerized all who gazed upon them.

"Hi, Vinny." Stephanie joyfully bounced into the front parlor. "How's business today? Any fresh meat?"

"Oh Steph, you are a funny one. I've told you that this is not a buffet. We are a legit business. A family business." Vinny continued processing his paperwork.

Her witchlike eyes scanned the room before she settled down on the comfy, velvet chair in the front gathering hall. Not a word was spoken out loud. Stephanie understood what Vinny was thinking. Her psychic abilities were strong and attuned to the world around her. A smile crept across her face as she gazed at the man before her. Her eyes traced the outline of his chiseled jawline. The way his short, black hair stood up in the front when it was cut too short. His long, dark lashes blinking rhythmically as he processed his work.

She knew he was documenting the intakes for the week, requesting death certificates, filling out processing reports and cremation certificates. His hands were strong. His forearm was decorated with a tattoo of a sword with a serpent wrapped around it. Many people wondered if a funeral ever actually happened at the numerous companies that filled the streets. Were they simply storefronts used to process the collateral damage of their "other family business"? Afterall, the Italian mob was alive and well in the City of Brotherly Love.

She sank back in the plush velvet chair in the front parlor of the funeral home. As she admired the man she loved, her thoughts drifted to his lineage. Vinny's family tree could be traced back to the great mobsters in Chicago's heyday.

The soft fabric caressed her skin and reminded her of sitting in the big, squishy chair as a child cuddled with her mom, Kaylee, as she read her favorite book. Where did she come from? It was always a mystery to her. She knew she was raised by her mother and she never really knew her father. She had distant memories of them in the mountains when she was around three, but that was it. It was something that Kaylee never wanted to discuss in much detail.

As a child, Stephanie would climb into her mother's lap and ask about her father. Kaylee always obliged. She would talk of his physical strength, his intelligence, his sense of humor. He was represented in a very positive light. She never had a negative thing to say. She often spoke of their trips to the mountains to see his grandparents.

Kaylee really loved his grandmother and grandfather. She would also add that she wished they had lived long enough to meet her, but God had other plans. Stephanie longed to know her father. She knew he was still alive, she could sense it. When she asked why he was not in their lives, Kaylee's response was always the same: "Sometimes things don't always work out as we hope. Perhaps one day, he will enter into our lives again, when the time is right."

The music played softly in the background and mostly went unnoticed. In the stillness of the moment, she found herself humming along to the song "My Favorite Things." She made up her own lyrics.

The Great Smoky Mountains and fishing in rivers
Sounds of the forest and sipping on whiskey
Sweet frozen treats that are served on a stick
These are a few of my favorite things

She sang quietly.

Spending time in the southern mountains of the Carolinas and Tennessee always held a special place in her heart. She felt more connected to something, to someone. She gained strength from the mountains. The history, the family that grew there. The voices were louder there, yet peaceful.

"A penny for your thoughts?" The deep, sexy, familiar voice brought her back into the present. "You always get in your trance when you sit in this room, especially on the velvet chairs."

"They wrap me in a warm hug. I feel safe." Stephanie smiled at Vinny. "Are you about done?"

"Just let me save these last things and send everything out. Then we're off to the races." He organized the files and placed the death certificate requests in the envelope. "Any preference where you want to go eat tonight? It is our last night in the city before heading off to Chicago."

"I could go for a cheesesteak."

"Can't think of a better last meal in Philly. Cheesesteaks it is." Vinny jumped up from his desk, walked over, leaned down, and gave her a kiss on the top of her head. "Let's get out of here."

"It must have rained while we were inside." The jingle of Vinny's keys as he locked the door mingled with the splashing of tires in the puddles on the street.

As they walked towards the sub shop, the smell of the spring evening rain filled the air. The clean, fresh scent signified rebirth as it cleansed the earth. The water ridded the world of all the dirt and filth of humanity. Allowed for peace and tranquility to filter in. The water ran down the gutters towards the sewers, carrying away the grime of the day. The oily residue formed color slicks as it approached the drain.

The sky above was speckled with clouds tinged orange and pink as the sun sank lower in the western horizon. Another perfect ending to a day here on earth. Soon the stars and moon would take over the sky and the demons in her head would stir again. Nighttime was not always pleasant.

The light of the full moon shone through the window as Stephanie and Vinny retired for the night. The sound of Vinny's rhythmic breathing calmed Stephanie, but even with her eyes closed the thoughts in her mind raced wildly.

She begged to still the waters of her mind. Stephanie slowed her breathing. She focused on mindful meditation practices for relaxation and peacefulness. Nothing seemed to work. The strength of the full moon energized her psyche. The spirits chatted wildly in her head but gave her no cause for alarm. This was normal.

Her spirit guide was a wise soul and often stepped forward to support her in time of struggle or crossroads. The flame from her bedside candle flickered in the darkness. Stephanie adjusted her pillow and propped herself up.

"If sleep will not come to me tonight, at least I can make use of the time," she whispered to herself.

Focused on her pending trip to Chicago, Stephanie channeled her spirit guide and asked for safe travel, patience, grace, and wisdom regarding the difficult conversation she planned to have with her mother. Stephanie has always been a very spiritual person. She had visions and psychic experiences since she was a small child. She was never scared of them, as they were always with her. Her main spirit guide was an older soul that she thought of as a grandmother figure. She was maternal, caring, wise, and nurturing.

She provided Stephanie with a sense of safety and belonging. Stephanie remembered having dreams as a small child of a woman with blonde hair and striking blue eyes and often with her was a boy with blonde hair and piercing blue eyes. As the years passed, the characters in the dream aged as well. When they came to her as she slept, she never saw the face of the boy. She saw the older woman, but never the boy. She had prayed for as long as she could remember to be shown the face of the boy in her dreams but to no avail. This faceless person haunted Stephanie her whole life, until recently.

A few months ago, she awoke abruptly from a sound sleep and remembered a clear vision of a face. She grabbed a sketch pad and drew out what she had seen. The chiseled face of a man. Strong jaw, light short hair. His eyes stuck in her mind. Perfectly shaped eyebrows framing his deep crystal-blue eyes with a hint of yellow around the pupil. Light reflected off his eyes and they sparkled like gems.

She felt a strong connection to this man, although she was fairly certain she had never met him before. What was the connection? She had her sketch and wanted to show it to her mother to see if she could shed any light on it. She knew it would be a difficult conversation. There were a lot of secrets about their past that her mother held close. Stephanie had never met anyone from her father's family, although she knew many of them through stories and had visited their hometowns. She longed to be able to touch them, to connect with them, to feel them. They shared the same lifeblood and a cosmic connection that could not be ignored.

Stephanie sensed this man and her grandmotherly spirit guide were part of her family. Only her mother could help her unravel this mystery and finally end her search for her father.

Stephanie and Vinny headed to the airport to catch their flight to Chicago early in the morning. Stephanie blinked repeatedly as she rubbed her eyes in a vain attempt to remove the sleepless night and replace it with refreshed, energized alertness. The sounds of people rushing to catch their impending flights filled the air.

Looking at the countless faces of the hurried travelers, she wondered where they were going. Were they headed to a remote vacation spot, a business trip to a faraway land, a trip back home to a loved one? She searched their eyes for a glimpse into their world, an escape from her own. She focused on one traveler specifically, as she stood out from the crowd and not only due to her brightly colored hair. The perfectly shaped curls hung in bouncy spirals around her face. She had a presence about her that resonated with Stephanie. Slowed to almost a stop, Stephanie stared at the woman as she expertly maneuvered through security, smiled, and offered quick banter with the TSA agents. Everyone seemed to take notice of her. Her aura was strong and inviting. Stephanie didn't know who she was, but she sensed that their paths would cross again, and she had much to learn from this young, attractive woman.

"Come on, Steph, you are holding up the line." Vinny's voice snapped her back into the task at hand.

"Sorry, I just got distracted." Stephanie rushed to put her bags on the conveyer.

They found their way to the gate. The airport speaker as it announced departing flights and searched for lost passengers punctuated her every step along the way. They boarded the plane and soon would arrive in Chicago. She dreaded the conversation with her mother. She slipped on her headphones as she blocked out the noise of the flight and the world.

Stephanie ran through the pending conversation in her head, over and over. She wrung her hands together as she tried to dry the moisture from them as she walked through different scenarios in her mind. She took deep breaths, closed her eyes tightly, blocked out the outside world, and retreated into the tranquility of her innermost thoughts.

Her ears popped, signifying the impending landing. Stephanie pulled out the drawing of the man she saw in her dreams. Who was he? Why did he haunt her so? Would her mother recognize him so she could finally put a name to the face? Her hands shook as she held the drawing, tilted her head back, and looked towards the sky as she searched for answers. Stephanie wished this would come to be.

Vinny and Stephanie made their way down the jet bridge, through the crowded airport, and finally passed through the security gates to freedom. They searched for that familiar face, with the striking green eyes and long, flowing hair. Stephanie spotted her mom, Kaylee, as she frantically waved her arm in the air to grab their attention. Stephanie's steps quickened as she rushed to meet her mother and fall into the safety of her arms. No matter how old she was, she always felt safest in her mother's arms. All of the anxiety that plagued her for the last few days disappeared.

"Welcome, you two! Don't you both look wonderful!" Kaylee gushed as she wrapped her arms around her grown daughter, kissing her cheek before she let go and reached for Vinny.

"So good to see you, Mom." Vinny hugged her tight. "It was a good flight, and I bet Steph is ready to grab a quick nap before we grab a late lunch."

Stephanie smiled at Vinny. "A little rest would do me some good. I got up very early."

"Let's get you guys back to the house so you can relax for a bit. The car is right outside."

———•———

Lying down on the soft bed, snuggled in the fluffy comforter, Stephanie hoped that sleep would not evade her yet again. Within a few moments, her wish was granted and she slept. Her face took on a peaceful appearance as the muscles around her eyes and mouth relaxed. Her breathing slowed, and her mind settled. Several hours later, she awoke, refreshed with a new outlook on things. She was ready to confront her demons. Today, she would know the truth.

The air around the table was thick with tension. The sounds of the silverware clanked as they struck the dishes. Finally, Vinny broke the silence.

"Kaylee, this is a great meal. You have certainly outdone yourself."

"Thank you, Vinny. Happy to hear you are enjoying it." Kaylee smiled.

"I do love a home-cooked meal. Stephanie is a great cook as well. I see where she gets her skills from." Vinny reached over and patted Stephanie's arm.

"Vinny has survived a few instances that didn't go as planned. That's for sure," Stephanie blushed a bit. "I enjoy experimenting a bit too much sometimes!"

Everyone laughed.

Stories of failed dinner attempts lightened the mood and gave them a focal point. The underlying realization that there were other items to discuss lingered in the back of Stephanie's mind and soon she would address the elephant in the room.

After dinner, Kaylee and Stephanie headed out to the back deck as the western sky lit up with splendid colors of red, orange, and pink as the sun dipped below the horizon. Vinny stayed behind and cleaned up the dishes and kitchen. He gave the ladies a bit of private time to talk.

Stephanie grabbed the sketchpad from her bag before heading outside.

"That certainly is a beautiful sunset," Kaylee commented.

"It sure is, Mom. Mother Nature has certainly done a good job painting the sky." Stephanie took a sip from her wineglass. She swished the wine around in her mouth for a moment and swallowed hard.

"Mom, lately I have been thinking a lot about family and Dad's side."

The words hung in the air, drifting around like the lingering odor after cooking fish. Kaylee scrunched up her nose a bit, took in a deep breath, and exhaled sharply at the scent the words left.

"I have always had these dreams as long as I can remember." She looked straight in her mother's eyes so she could gauge her reaction. "They have the same people in them, but I don't know who they are. We've talked about them and how they are my spirit guides."

Kaylee nodded in affirmation, signaling Stephanie to continue.

"These spirit guides have always had another person with them that I have not mentioned to you." Kaylee rubbed her fingers across the cover of the sketchbook that contained the portrait of the unknown face.

"Until recently, this person never had a face. I knew it was a male figure, but they were faceless." Her voice trembled as she spoke quietly. "When I was young, I wondered if it was a relative and I would pretend that it was my father and the lady was my grandmother, this little boy's mother."

Her eyes rose to meet her mother's. She searched for some sign of acceptance of the confession that Stephanie was about to make. A smile crept across her face as Kaylee reached out, placing her hand on her daughter's.

The warmth of her mother's hand radiated through Stephanie and she knew that this was a safe place. She felt the presence of her maternal spirit guide. The support in both the current tangible world as well as the spiritual one gave her strength to continue.

"For my whole life, I never saw his face, but the other week, I did." Tears rolled down her cheeks. "It was so vivid and his eyes were so striking. The eyes are the windows to our souls and Deb showed me his eyes and his face. I felt a connection to this person and somehow they were someone I knew or will know. Someone very important in my journey here on earth."

Kaylee's eyes grew large and she gasped at the mention of Deb.

"Mom, are you okay?"

She took a second to compose herself. "Wh-wh-why did you say Deb? Is that the name of your spirit guide?" Kaylee struggled with the words.

"Yes." Stephanie was slightly confused by her mother's reaction. "I rarely refer to her by name, but that is what she calls herself. There is another man with her, normally a much older spirit, he presents himself as Darryl."

"Oh, Steph," Kaylee's voice trembled as she struggled to get the words out. "Deb is the name of your paternal grandmother. I never met her. She passed away suddenly before I met your father."

Stephanie's eyes were locked on her mother as she searched for signs of more information. "And Darryl?"

"Darryl was her father. Your father's grandfather, your great-grandfather," Kaylee answered.

"Did you know him?"

"Oh yes! Pappy, as we called him, was a wonderful man. I knew him and your great-grandmother Martha Mason as well. They were lovely people. Lived in Tennessee, as you know." Kaylee's eyes brightened as she continued to talk about Pappy and Martha.

Stephanie's eyes sparkled as she listened to her mother talk about happy times at the homestead and her travels to their home in Tennessee. She included references to Curtis, Stephanie's father. The stories painted a Norman Rockwell facade of her time with her father and his family. She sprinkled in memories of home-cooked meals, drinking moonshine around the campfire, and tales of Tucker, their dog. Stephanie remembered Tucker from when she was a child.

Stephanie knew her mother well. Over the years, she realized that conversations concerning Curtis were always superficial. Something always was held back. She needed to know what this was and why Deb and Darryl showed her this man.

Stephanie reached for the folder and rubbed her hands across it.

"Mom, I want to show you something else. I drew a picture of the face," Stephanie whispered as she treaded lightly into the difficult point of the conversation. "The man that has been with them in my dreams."

Kaylee straightened her back, sat tall in her chair, and took a deep breath. She nodded for Stephanie to continue.

Her hand opened the folder slowly and reached for the drawing. She held it for a moment, studying the face before she turned it around and silently slid it across the table towards her mother.

Stephanie was focused on her mother's reaction. She was able to control her words but not her initial emotional response.

Kaylee's eyes were closed. Slowly, she opened them to reveal the drawing Stephanie had laid before her. As her eyes began to focus on the pencil lines forming the outline of a face, a familiar face, the tears began to roll down her cheeks.

"That is your father," was all Kaylee said in a hushed tone.